MILTON

TRACY LYNN

WORKBOOK PRESS LLC
187 E Warm Springs Rd,
Suite B285 Las Vegas NV 89119 USA

Website: https://workbookpress.com/
Hotline: 1-888-818-4856
Email: admin@workbookpress.com

Ordering Information:

Quantity sales. Special discounts are available on quantity purchases by corporations, associations, and others. For details, contact the publisher at the address above.

Library of Congress Control Number:
ISBN-13:   978-1-965732-66-3   Paperback Version
                978-1-965732-67-0   Digital Version

REV. DATE: 07/23/2025

CONTENTS

CHAPTER 1

London, 1863

Mrs. Shaw had always been a part of high society. She had been born into a well-to-do family, and when she married Sir John, she had married into wealth as well. At times, Sir John had made bad financial choices that she had to bear the weight of, which was common in a society of men. When she was young, she had always imagined that she would have wealth, and the thought of never having it had never crossed her mind. She had also supposed that on the day she married, her husband would be a wealthy man, and that would be more important than love. Now, thinking about how her sister had suffered because of her choice of man, she thought, Ifonly Marie hadmadethesamedecisionasIdidinmymarriage. But no, Marie had married for love. Mrs. Shaw had not been in love with Mr. Shaw when she had married him. His position in society had been what was most important to her at the time. Look where Marie had ended up. She had gone to Milton with Mr. Hale and her daughter, Margaret, and had gotten ill because of her worries and ended up dying for it. Mr. Hale had highly misjudged the circumstances he had put his family into by moving there. He had left the church and the security it had provided for them in Helstone to move the family to Milton. This had put them through a change that had lowered their financial circumstances to such a degree that they were taken to a lower level of society. He had caused the whole family to suffer ridicule from others, and that had caused unhappiness in Marie. Frankly, it had been appalling to take them to a smoky town like Milton. I can't believe that he would have turned his back on the church and taken them to such a place, thought Mrs. Shaw to herself. It had been bad enough after the incident with Frederick, their son. The mutiny that had happened on his ship that Frederick had been involved in against the captain of the ship! Poor Marie had written to her to explain her great remorse and sadness at the event.

Mrs. Shaw had thought nothing else could possibly happen, but she had been wrong. She had told herself that was why she had married for the monetary value and companionship, not for love, though she had envied Marie for finding it. Marie had always been of a delicate condition, and marrying Mr. Hale, a clergyman, had made sense at the time. Marie had blossomed with her love for him. But Marie hadn't realized at the time the potential strain of a clergyman's life. She hadn't realized that the money given to them by the parish might not help them to totally care for all of the community's needs. Sometimes the food or live animals given to the poor came through donations made by others in the community as well as by the parish and the Hales. They lived a little way from the others in their community, and Marie had complained about this quite often to Mrs. Shaw. Marie had felt waves of loneliness at living so far from others in the community, but helping the less fortunate had always raised her spirits and given her a sense of purpose. Mrs. Shaw knew that life had seemed hard to Marie since she had written as much in her letters to Mrs. Shaw over those restless years. Mr. Shaw, when he had died, had left Mrs. Shaw quite well taken care of through investments and wagers. There had been no great debt caused from his death, so Mrs. Shaw and their daughter, Edith, had been well provided for. Edith's wedding, though a great cost, had been brought right by the fact that Captain Lennox made quite a good living and could provide Edith's every need. Edith loved Captain Lennox a great deal and after the birth of two children had made Mrs. Shaw an even better grandmother. Mrs. Shaw could provide—if the day should ever arise—for her grandchildren if they needed it. She set up a fund for them through Henry, who would oversee everything for her. Henry, being Edith's brother- in-law, had always come into Mrs. Shaw's mind as a terrific catch for Margaret, her niece. He was well put up and had a bright-looking future as a barrister. Mr. Thornton. arriving yesterday to the dinner party with Henry, had done little to change Mrs. Shaw's mind. Mr. Thornton had been an acquaintance of Margaret's, to be sure, while she had lived in Milton. It had been over a year since she had seen him, but she had not showed any outward signs of it being more than that. Mrs. Shaw had held the dinner party on schedule with her annual plans. Although she didn't hold men like Mr. Thornton, whom she considered a tradesman, in too high regard, she did have to admit that he was decent at what he did.

Little did she know what had been going on in her house on the very day these many thoughts had been chasing each other in her mind. Mrs. Shaw had been at the Pipers' for her weekly visit. The Pipers were a wealthy family of musicians who came from family money and had built their own music center to perform in called the Piper Center. Mrs. Shaw enjoyed going to the center greatly. She had only been saddened that Margaret hadn't wanted to come with her and Edith to listen to them. Mrs. Shaw sat there listening to the music and thinking her thoughts, daydreaming about a match between Henry and her niece. *What a great day that will be when Henry asks the question!* thought Mrs. Shaw. She only wished she could be there to see it. It could even happen this very day! Had they not left the house on Harley Street just as Henry was arriving in a carriage? Mrs. Shaw smiled as she imagined it. Henry would get down on one knee, hold Margaret's hand, and kiss it as he asked her to be his for the rest of their lives. Mrs. Shaw envisioned Margaret's response. "Henry, I knew you would ask me one day!" Margaret would reply. Henry would tell her sweet nothings, and they would come to ask for her blessing. Mrs. Shaw would gladly give it too. There could not be a better match for Margaret than Henry. Captain Lennox and Edith would be so excited and would go on about the wedding preparations. *I could help plan it all,* thought Mrs. Shaw. There would be no expense spared. Margaret would have the best, even more than her mother had had. Mr. Bell had been quite generous in making Margaret his sole beneficiary after her father had died and before he himself had died. Mrs. Shaw praised him for it. Mr. Bell had been prudent with his choice of Margaret and so kind, as her godfather, to provide for her in such a generous way.

Edith nudged Mrs. Shaw, bringing her out of her thoughts, and asked, "Mother, you haven't been listening, have you?"

"Oh, I'm sorry, dear. I can't help but think that Henry might propose to Margaret today!" whispered Mrs. Shaw.

"Oh, do you really think so? Has he said something to you about it?" Edith whispered.

"No, it's just that he said he had a meeting with Margaret today about business. But I think that was just an excuse to get her alone to ask her."

"That would be great for us all," said Edith, and then paused. "Margaret could live close to us, or even with us, couldn't she?"

"I don't know if Henry and Margaret would want to live with you," said Mrs. Shaw, smiling at her. "They may want their privacy." She winked at her daughter and smiled as she turned to enjoy the Pipers' music. They had been here almost an hour, but she didn't want to leave before she thought Henry would have had time to propose to Margaret and take her in his arms. Edith pointed to a young lady in the back of the room. "Mother, is that not Mary Hurley, the old barrister's daughter? You know, the one who works with Henry?"

"You know, I believe it is," said Mrs. Shaw, holding her glasses to her eyes to get a better look.

"I have heard she has taken a fancy to a carriage-maker's son," said Edith. "Well, surely her father won't approve of that," said Mrs. Shaw. "Besides,

she has her position in society to think about!"

"I think it hardly matters what her father thinks. I have heard she is very strong-minded and will do what she wants," Edith noted with an amused smile.

Mrs. Shaw studied the Hurley girl for several moments and came to the conclusion that the girl didn't show the proper airs for society anyway. She probably would do very well for a carriage-maker's son after all, even though her father was a barrister and had the means to make it a really nice wedding, full of all the things that his daughter could ever possibly want or need at such an event. They could also have simple wedding plans and make it more appropriate for a carriage-maker's son by use of more casual decorations and flowers. *Yes,* Mrs. Shaw thought, *that really could go either way, and society will neither notice nor care.*

Back at the house on Harley Street, Margaret and Mr. Thornton had been in the study discussing her business proposal to invest in

Mr. Thornton's cotton mill, which she now owned, when they had come to the simultaneous realization that the only thing standing in the way of their love for each other had been a mutually selfish pride. He had thought she was in love with the stranger at Outwood Station. She had thought she had driven him away forever because of her prior rejection of his marriage proposal.

"I want you to know that I only turned you down at the time because I was afraid for my mother's health and my father's needs," said Margaret. "I also couldn't stand the way you treated others," she added wryly. "But now I know better. I didn't understand everything about the situation with the workers."

"I was shattered first by your refusal, and then thought it was because of the man at Outwood Station," said John. "Why didn't you trust me enough to tell me it was your brother?"

"Frederick was involved in a mutiny, and coming to England was a great risk to his life!" Margaret explained. "I didn't know if he had made it back to Spain, and I couldn't risk him getting caught because of me."

"Why would it have been because of you?"

"I was the one who wrote to tell him of mother's illness. It was my fault that he came back to England," said Margaret.

"He would have wanted to be here. Surely your father and mother told you that?"

"Yes, Father did say he was glad I was brave enough to do it. But then when that man saw Frederick at the station, I thought he would be caught for sure! Thank goodness you covered for me. I can never thank you enough for doing that," said Margaret.

"Even if I did deny it to you at the time, I still cared so deeply for you, in fact more so because of you rejecting my proposal." John smiled down at her. Taking her hand in his, he pulled it up to his lips and tenderly laid a kiss upon it. "I adore your small, soft hands," he murmured. "They are so delicate and lovely, just like you."

Mrs. Shaw and Edith came out of the Pipers and made their way through the crowd to the carriage where Captain Lennox was waiting for them. Captain Lennox had been taking care of some business on the other side of London but had returned to escort the ladies home. "The music was lovely today," said Mrs. Shaw as Captain Lennox put out his hand to help her into the carriage.

"Mary Hurley was there," said Edith, distractedly excited about the possibility of a wedding soon when she thought of Margaret and Henry.

"Some of the ladies' garments were a little inappropriate for the event, though," said Mrs. Shaw, looking at the Captain.

"I have often thought why should it matter so much what one wears to those things? After all, you are just there to listen," said the Captain, immediately noticing the look of disagreement on Mrs. Shaw's face.

"Oh, don't tease Mother so," said Edith, smiling at him. "She will always state her opinion on the circumstances she finds herself in, and I for one think it a great quality to her character."

"Then I can only say I'm sorry and leave it at that. I shall never tease you again," said Captain Lennox, lifting Mrs. Shaw's hand and kissing it delicately. Mrs. Shaw glanced up at him and blushed.

"Now you've made her blush and me jealous," said Edith, pretending to pout, but smiling to herself at the kindness he had shown to her mother.

They continued down the thoroughfare to Harley Street where they spotted Dixon returning to the house from her shopping. She had her arms full of parcels and was waiting for the butler, Edmunds, to open the service door. As Dixon stepped inside the doorway, the carriage pulled up to the front of the house, and the ladies and Captain Lennox stepped out of the carriage and came up the steps to the front door. Margaret and Mr. Thornton were just coming out of the study as the three of them entered the hallway. Edith looked at Margaret's face and then at Mr. Thornton's. She noticed something there, but wasn't quite sure what. Margaret proceeded to make introductions as Captain Lennox reached around Edith to shake Mr. Thornton's hand. "It's nice to see you again. It has been a while since the exhibition, hasn't it?" asked Captain Lennox, smiling.

"It has been a while," said Mr. Thornton.

The gentlemen retired to the sitting room to wait while the ladies refreshed themselves for teatime. Mrs. Shaw was frowning as she went to her room to change. Edith took Margaret's arm and headed for their rooms upstairs. "So, tell me, cousin. What did you and Mr. Thornton have to talk about? Did he come to talk about the business? I know you had to discuss some things with him about the mill."

"Yes, the business discussions went quite well," said Margaret, deciding to wait to tell her and the others about Mr. Thornton and herself until after teatime. Margaret remembered that Edith had always been a delicate child when she had come to live with her aunt and cousin at the age of nine. Margaret had always been told to be gentle with Edith, and that she was to be treated like a fine China doll that no one was to break. Edith could be strong at times, however. She had shown that to everyone when she married Captain Lennox and had their children. One of the boys dearly loved Margaret, and he loved for Margaret to read to him.

Margaret considered herself plain looking, but she thought Edith was beautiful, with blond hair and creamy skin and her eyes a light shade of blue, like the sky in the height of the morning, filled with light. Edith spent her days in leisure, either going to society functions or being with the children. The children had a nanny who watched them most of the time, but Edith loved her children and doted on them. Edith always said, "They need a good education so they will know the business world." The boys flourished under her guidance. Captain Lennox taught the boys things that only a father knew to teach them, things about the world in general. As they reached Edith's room, Margaret mused that Edith had done a fine job with her family.

"I'll meet you downstairs for tea," Margaret said as she went on down the hallway and opened the door to her own small, comfortable room. Margaret thought about how she was going to break the news to everyone. They would all be shocked, except for Henry. He probably suspected something by now. Edith would cry at her leaving, and Mrs. Shaw would be the hardest to tell, as she had such a superior attitude in such matters. Margaret quickly changed into a fresh dress and fixed her hair. As she looked in the mirror, she wondered at what John saw in her. Her whole life, people had told her she was rather plain looking. She thanked John in her heart for never saying as much to anyone. She smiled at her reflection, remembering the kiss John had given her. Her heart was overflowing with love for the man, and she wasn't sure if she would be able to hold her countenance while at tea. She entered the hallway just as Edith was coming out of her room. They walked together to the sitting room where the tea was to be served and found everyone waiting for them, including Mr. Thornton. Margaret smiled at him as she entered the room. Mrs. Shaw started asking Mr. Thornton questions about the mill and the people of Milton while Edith directed her attention to Margaret.

"Tell me about Mr. Thornton. What is he like, Margaret?"

"Well, you already know he is a manufacturer and that he runs a cotton mill in Milton," said Margaret. "In fact, if you remember, that is what the business meeting was about today."

"What do you want to do with his cotton works anyway?" asked Edith, shocked at the prospect of being around that kind of thing.

"The mill in Milton was willed to me by Mr. Bell, so with the money I have now, I want to invest in running the mill."

"Does that mean you would go back there from time to time?"

"Yes, I suppose it does," said Margaret, seeing the horrified look on Edith's face. "It's really not all that bad there," she added, trying to soothe her cousin.

"Well, at least it won't be often," said Edith, looking over at Captain Lennox and smiling at him. Mr. Thornton, overhearing their conversation, chimed in.

"Mrs. Lennox, Milton is the best manufacturing town in the North. I promise you that your cousin will be quite safe when she comes there!"

Mrs. Shaw gave a doubtful glance to Margaret and Mr. Thornton. "Where is Henry?" she asked Margaret. "I thought he was arriving for the meeting today. Just as we were leaving, I saw a carriage coming to the house."

"I guess he had some business that detained him because he never came.

So I just conducted the meeting without him," said Margaret.

Mrs. Shaw looked sternly at her. "Margaret, you were all alone in a room with a man? Just what were you thinking?"

"I didn't sense any danger from Mr. Thornton or I wouldn't have done it," said Margaret, growing irritated. "Besides, if I had sensed any danger, I could have called for a servant." She felt like laughing, despite her irritation, but held it back so as not to offend her aunt.

"She was fine, Mrs. Shaw. The pillar of decorum," said Mr. Thornton, though if anyone but Margaret had noticed, his eyes were holding back the laughter as well.

Captain Lennox gave his wife a smile and looked to Mr. Thornton. "Do you think we men should go to the garden while the ladies tittle-tattle among themselves?" John nodded his head at him, motioning for them to take their leave. He glanced back as they left the room, hoping that Margaret wouldn't have too hard of a time explaining everything to her cousin and aunt.

Teatime was over, and Margaret had the chance to finally talk to Edith and Mrs. Shaw. Margaret was getting ready to tell them the news when one of he boys could be heard crying down the hall. Edith excused herself and went to check on them. Margaret turned to her aunt and said, "I have some good news to tell you."

"What is it, my dear? I could tell during teatime that you wanted to tell us all something."

Margaret looked at her aunt nervously. "I don't know exactly where to start, but I need to tell you that I am in love, and I am getting married."

Mrs. Shaw put her hands to her mouth to muffle a scream of excitement. She reached over and gave Margaret a big hug. "Oh, my dear, I knew it would happen. I knew he would finally get up the courage to ask you!" she exclaimed. Margaret started to smile as her aunt continued. "So have Henry and you set a date?"

Margaret instantly lost her smile. "What are you talking about, Aunt? I am not marrying Henry! I am marrying Mr. Thornton!"

Mrs. Shaw stood up from her chair, frowning and distant, and walked over to look out the window. "How can you consider marrying that man?" she finally asked, her voice dripping with disdain.

"To be quiet honest, I didn't think I would ever marry," said Margaret. "But, Aunt, he has the kindest heart. If you only knew of all the kindnesses he has shown my family." Margaret turned away from her aunt, casting a downward glance. "I am a woman of property now, and I am free to make my own decisions. He is what I want. I love him and have loved him for a while now," she said softly.

Mrs. Shaw turned from the window. "What are these kindnesses you speak of?"

"Frederick came to see us while Mother lay dying. We kept it a secret, of course." Margaret started pacing around the room. "But then a situation arose involving a man Frederick knew from before. When we were at the station, the night he was to leave, this situation caused us to send him to London rather quickly. He was coming to see Henry anyway for help with his case against the Captain." She paused. "John saw Frederick with me at the station that night and kept it a secret from all of Milton."

"What situations arose?" Mrs. Shaw asked, pulling Margaret down to sit beside her on the sofa.

"There was a young man who had known Frederick from Helstone. He recognized Frederick and got into an altercation with him. The man later died, although Frederick didn't cause his death. But I was questioned about it by the police. Someone else at the station had witnessed me being there. John, being the magistrate of Milton, had the case stopped due to lack of medical evidence." Mrs. Shaw looked at her, still puzzled. "You see, Aunt, I had denied being at the station at the time the man died, so John lied for me."

Mrs. Shaw's face lit with understanding. "Oh, I see." She patted Margaret's arm. "He deserves you then. But I still wish you didn't have to go back to that smoky place."

Margaret touched her aunt's hand. "I have grown to love the cotton mill and the people living in Milton. It's only right for me to be where John is."

As Margaret stood to leave, Edith entered the room, her face stained with tears. "Margaret, tell me it's not true, that you're not leaving us to go back to Milton."

"Yes, I must, Edith, although I am sorry to leave you. I am traveling with John on the next train to Milton," said Margaret. "And we are to be married soon as well."

Edith looked into her cousin's face and saw the light in her eyes. It was the happiest she had seen Margaret since the death of Mr.

Bell and her parents. "Oh, Margaret, I shall miss you so! But I can tell you have to go, and he is so lucky to have won your heart, my dear cousin."

"I rather think I am the lucky one," said Margaret, thinking of John and how her pride had almost caused her his love. John and Captain Lennox walked in the room as the Captain was giving John his blessing on the marriage. "Next to my wife, she is the finest lady I have ever known," said Captain Lennox, shaking John's hand. Mr. Thornton smiled and turned his attention to Margaret. He walked over to her as the others started chatting with one another.

Taking her hand in his, he asked, "How are you holding up?"

She looked up at him and said, "I'm quite relieved to have told my aunt. She has given her blessing." She smiled at him and raised his hand to kiss it. Margaret gazed into his eyes, wondering why she had never realized the love that burnt for her there. She felt she could get lost in his gaze forever. John was returning her gaze and wondering how his mother was going to react to the news. How had Margaret put it when she had referred to John's mother's quote? Ah, yes. "That woman!" Would she respect Margaret for finally realizing her son's worth? Or would she regret it because she was losing him to another? As if sensing his feelings, Margaret said, "Hopefully she will understand in time." John smiled, still unable to believe she was going back with him. He had truly never loved anyone but his mother until now. At this moment, he thought himself the luckiest man on all the earth to have found her. To know she loved him in return made him glad that he had never given up on her even when it had seemed hopeless to him.

Margaret left to go pack her things as John found the butler to order a ride for them. Margaret's servant, Dixon, was standing by Margaret's dresser, holding the missus brooch that Margaret had inherited on her mother death. "I remember the first time I saw the missus wear this," said Dixon. "It was at the charity ball for Mary Dom Ville's little boy. Your mother had invited everyone she could think of to raise money for him. He was such a little thing to get so sick so soon in life. Isn't it a wonder he survived it all?" Smiling, Margaret went to select her clothes to pack. Dixon turned to her, fumbling with a day dress. "Miss, I'm sorry, but I can't go back there. I can't stand that smoky place! I wanted to go for you, but I just can't. There's too many bad memories for me there." She noticed the look on Margaret's face and tried not to weep. "I'm so sorry, Miss, and I know it was bad for you too. But now you will have joy." She touched Margaret on

the shoulder.

Margaret put down a dress and turned to Dixon. "I'm going to be fine, Dixon, and I won't force you to go if your heart is set on staying here. I will learn to carry on without you. I know you'll be happier here anyway." Margaret smiled at Dixon and gave her a kiss on the cheek.

"Bless you, Miss. Bless you and your new life." Dixon finished putting the jewelry into a box and handed it to Margaret. Margaret took the box and put it in her bag.

"I guess it's time to say good-bye," said Margaret, as she finished the packing. "I will miss you, Dixon." She gave her maid a hug.

"Me too, Miss," said Dixon as she left the room, wiping her eyes. Margaret gave the room one last look. It seemed it had been her room forever, and now a part of her would miss it. Margaret closed the door and went down the hallway to the stairs to return to the others. John was waiting at the bottom of the stairs for her. As she reached him, Henry was announced by the butler and immediately came to her side.

"I need to talk to you!" Henry exclaimed, grabbing her hand to pull her into the now-empty study and closing the door behind them. John was left standing there, frowning at the way Henry had grabbed her.

He started to open the study door when Captain Lennox stopped him with a hand on his arm. "He has burned a torch for her for a long time now, John."

"That is all well and good, but did you see the way he grabbed her? That isn't the act of a gentleman."

"I know, but he's upset. Wouldn't you be if you were him?" asked Captain Lennox.

"I see what you mean, but at least check on them to make sure she is well!"

Captain Lennox peeked into the doorway. Henry seemed to have calmed down. "Everything appears to be fine," he told John as he returned to the foyer. John leaned against the hall wall, tucking his hands into his pockets and feeling the crystal face of his father's watch as he waited for his beloved to resolve the issue with Henry.

Henry was standing, looking down at Margaret, and asked her to take a seat. "I need to explain something to you. I know you think you love this Thornton man. But there are some things you may not know about him. He hasn't always been as well off as when you first met him, for one."

"Yes, Henry, I already know that," said Margaret, taking a seat. "Did you know his father killed himself?" asked Henry bluntly.

"Yes, as a matter of fact, I did. My father told me all about it when we first moved to Milton."

"Then how can you be considering him? Don't you think it shows what kind of family he comes from?" asked Henry.

"What his father did has no bearing on the kind of person John is!" "Margaret, he has nothing now except what your money can do for him." "I can't believe you would say such a thing!" exclaimed Margaret. She

stood up, wringing her hands at Henry's harsh tone.

"Well, why else would he be asking you to marry him now?"

"Because he loves me!" Margaret yelled at him. "You know nothing about his character or his responsibilities! Besides, what makes you think he hadn't already asked me to marry him, *before* his business suffered?"

"Well, did he?" asked Henry.

"Yes, he did! Back in Milton, before Mother or Father died!" Margaret's eyes gleamed with tears and anger.

Henry's face showed his confusion. "But you refused him then?"

"Yes, Henry, because of my pride," she replied, her temper suddenly gone. "He is a wonderful man, with a great deal of responsibility and concern for his workers." She returned to her seat.

Henry suddenly understood that Margaret's mind was firm on this subject and that there was no way he would ever be dearest in her heart, not now, not ever. Her heart belonged to someone else, and he would have to grieve over his loss of her in his own way. "Well, I wish you all the best," he said finally. "And if you need my assistance in finances, you know how to reach me." There was nothing for it but to exit with as much grace as he had left. He opened the study door, grabbed his cover, and left the house, saying a hasty good-bye to his brother, Edith, and Mrs. Shaw on his way out.

John was still leaning against the wall, waiting, when Margaret came out. He looked at Henry's hasty departure and turned to Margaret. "Is everything well?" asked John, touching her hand.

"He isn't happy with my choice of you rather than him," said Margaret, faintly smiling. "I hate to cause him pain, but it is you I love." Margaret's sadness over the possible loss of a friend showed in her eyes.

"He will learn to deal with it!" John said, rather unfeelingly. But with another look at Margaret's face, he apologized for being so blunt with his statement. Mrs. Shaw and Edith stepped forward to say their good-byes to Margaret.

"I will miss you, Margaret, but I will see you soon, at your wedding," said Edith. "I will think of you until then." Margaret squeezed her hands tightly.

"Safe journey, my dears," Mrs. Shaw said with a kiss on Margaret's cheek. John helped her into the carriage before climbing in himself. Margaret waved to Edith as they pulled out onto the thoroughfare and mentally said farewell to the streets of London as they rode.

John turned to her as they reached the station. "So you're really coming home with me." He smiled as he teased her. Margaret returned the smile happily and followed him onto the train. Words were not necessary. When they had sat down, Margaret glanced at him and John leaned over to her and kissed her softly on the lips. Margaret wasn't sure of anything her heart was telling her except that she loved John. She glanced out the window as the train made its way out of the station and toward her new life.

CHAPTER 2

They had been traveling for a while when a whistle blew and the train began to slow down. John, who had been reading the newspaper, glanced over the news to look out the window. They were certainly not yet to Milton, he knew. Margaret, he noticed, had laid her head back and fallen asleep. He stood up and leaned over her to get a better view outside. There appeared to be a wagon with its wheel broken blocking the tracks. As the train slowed even more, Margaret woke up. "What's going on?" she asked, sitting up.

"It's a broken-down wagon on the tracks," said John. "It shouldn't take too long, and we'll be back on our way." He smiled down at her.

Margaret smiled back. "Was the news interesting in the paper?" She had noticed it in his hand.

"Oh, it was quite enlightening," said John. "I have found out that cotton manufacturing is going to be in even more demand than before due to new businesses starting up and new inventions happening to make the work more productive. There is a big want for more lightweight cotton products too instead of the woolen ones. And," he continued, "the silk industry seems to be doing quite well also."

"That is truly wonderful to hear," said Margaret, happy that if she was to be a businesswoman, at least her business of choice had a good future. As the train started up once again and headed on down the tracks, John almost fell into her lap as the train started picking up speed. They both started laughing, and Margaret told him, "That's what happens when you try to leave my side." He moved in closer to her and put his arm around her as they stared out the window at the sun starting to set. Margaret leaned back against his shoulder and put her hand on his, glad to be alone in their section of the train. "That sunset is so beautiful," she said as she gazed at the reds, oranges, and dark yellows in the sky. John was watching as the fading light was playing across the clouds, thinking how beautiful the reflection of the fading light looked across the surface of Margaret's hair, making it look almost a dark chestnut brown with reddish highlights. Margaret, noting his silence, asked about his thoughts.

"I was just admiring the scenery," he said, almost whispering. He leaned down and kissed the top of her head. He would always remember these quiet moments spent with her, and as the years past, he would understand her more and more. He was sure of that, as he felt so at home with her already. Hours later, when the train pulled into the station, Margaret glanced up at John as he was getting their bags.

"I'm almost afraid to see your mother again. She's not going to handle this news very well, especially after the way I rejected your earlier offer of marriage. I do hope you will forgive me," said Margaret, rather sadly.

Turning back to her, John said, "Don't you know I already have? I love you, silly girl. I can forgive anything as long as I have your love." John looked into her teary eyes, holding back the tears in his.

Margaret caught his hand as he turned to leave and reached up and turned his face back to hers to kiss him. That was all it took. She clung to him in a kiss and tasted the tears running down his cheek. She stopped to wipe away the tears, and putting both hands on his face, she said, "I will always love you, John Thornton. You are where my heart belongs, and I will never doubt that." John reached up and brushed away her tears as well, choking his emotions back into control.

Margaret took his arm as they stepped from the train. As they walked out into the station, memories flooded both their minds. They took the stairs to the street below and hailed Finn, the overseer, to take them to the house. Both remembered Frederick leaving and how John had mistaken her brother for a suitor that was in his way. They sat in silence as the carriage made its way down the dark thoroughfares. Margaret gazed out the window of the carriage, making out the figure of a small boy begging in the street for shilling and pence, bringing back the harsh realities of the workers' lives and of the time and place they lived in. When Margaret had come here to live with her family almost three years ago, she had been struck by how dirty and smoky the town appeared. The streets had been filled with people going about their different tasks, busily making their way through the smoke to this job or that. Margaret had looked out the window in disgust then, but not now. Now she understood the town as she was learning to understand its people, and most of all, she was learning to understand the pride in a town like this, a town of industry.

The street candles were burning bright as they made their way down High Street. The clouds of smoke from the day's work could be seen in the night sky. Some of the houses were already lit with candles burning inside as families came together after a long day's work. Margaret wondered what life was like for some of those houses. Was the family surviving their harsh life? Were they content in their path of life, although poor? Were they happy to be part of this industry of cotton and to have to deal with all its problems? The little boy in the street was only one example of how desperate a family could get in this day of industry and manufacturing, where wages were low and you had to scrounge for what you could get, sometimes working more than one job.

John had felt the lengths that men would go to help their own families when he had pulled his family out of poverty to where they were now. His company, Marlborough Mill, had been in business for at least ten years and had managed to stay above board in its costs, but strikes had taken a toll and bouts of illness among the workers had slowed production at times as well. John's mother had helped him keep the business operating. She understood the factory almost as well as John did. They employed about 450 workers, the majority of whom were children and women. The men would work the spinning mules, as it required great strength, and the women worked doing the weaving on the smaller equipment. The children would go under the equipment to catch falling cotton and to fix broken threads to the machines. The most dangerous part for the children was picking up the loose cotton pieces from under the spinning mules. The spinning mules moved at a high speed, and there was too much money to be lost if they were turned off while the children picked up the pieces. Quite often, children were injured or even killed doing this task. If the child died, there would often be no compensation given to the family for the loss of the position or for the loss of the child. There was also the problem of illness due to breathing in the fibers of the cotton that floated through the air in the sorting rooms, but it couldn't be helped.

John had gotten a better wheel to try to keep the cotton out of the air. It had helped but hadn't totally solved the problems associated with the cotton works. John had also told Margaret of rumors from Scotland several years before when a few men had actually attacked some of the women who were strong enough to work the mules, feeling their jobs were being threatened. The men had beaten the factory owners as well. Because of that, John had strict rules that only men ran the spinning mules in his factory and would not accept any complaints from his female workers about it.

Marlborough Mill stood to the side of the town and was a fair distance removed from Crampton where Margaret had lived with her mother and father when they had first moved to Milton. Crampton was an area of the poor and had dirty streets filled with people selling their wares, whether it be the butcher or fabrics, baskets or coal. The people crowded the streets with busy intentions. The more well-to-do citizens would come to Crampton for their shopping. The shilling and pence was the way of the streets, and you had to have shillings and pence in order to do business there. The houses in the area were cluttered and close to one another, with several families often together in one dwelling. There was always smoke from the mills blowing through the streets in Crampton, and sometimes the air was hard to breath. One had to be careful not to get sick or wet while out during the day because it could lead to colds and such. Margaret had liked their home there, even though there had been bad memories as well. She also had some good memories of the area. Nicholas and Mary, friends from her previous time in Milton, lived down on Francis Street, which was only a short way through the cemetery, passing by the church and down to the bottom of the hill. Margaret had usually enjoyed her walk to their home, which was located in the poorest part of the town. The streets there were hung with lines to hang one's clothes on to dry, and the byways were very narrow. The workers of the factories who lived in this area were often seen in the narrow back alleys cooking or boiling either things to eat or to clean. Some of the women dyed cloth for some of the factories before it was shipped off to be sold. The dyed cloth would hang on lines to dry, dripping dye into the streets and causing the colored water to run down the streets and into the waterways, coloring the rivers with dye that would turn a person's skin the same color if you put your hand into the water of the river. This particular area where Nicholas's house was located sat behind a tavern called the Golden Dragon, where the local menfolk would go for a pint on the weekends or even during the week if the day had been especially hard. Nicholas was often seen at the Golden Dragon by fellow workers who were all trying their best to deal with their circumstances of life. Nicholas was a committeeman, heading the union for the workers. He had additional stress because he had to maintain order among the workers, and sometimes they got unruly and he had to have meetings with them to calm them down. Many of the workers were very dissatisfied with their wages and lot in life. Nicholas was a good, steady man, but he was also a poor one. John had done some things to try to make it easier on his workers, but he also felt he needed to make profits for his family to survive as well.

High Street was the main thoroughfare in Milton, leading to the mill and their home. Margaret remembered the day the workers had attacked the gates of the mill and how she had gotten hurt. John had not backed down, and although the workers protested, they secretly admired John for his unbending standards for the mill. Marlborough Mill had a reputation for being the finest mill in the area with the best working conditions of all the mills. There were nineteen other mills in which the people of the town worked. John was magistrate of five of them, with four other magistrates in the town. Of the five magistrates, John oversaw the area and other mills surrounding his own. Nathan Hamper of Hampers Mill was a man who showed signs of weakness, but his brother Horatio had taken over for him, helping him run the mill. They had an overseer who was brutal to the workers. There was Henderson's Mill, which was a more decent place for the workers. There was Slickson's Mill, which had an owner of general debauchery and cruelty who tried to get away with all kinds of unseemly things with his workers. There was Wilson's Mill, which had just reopened recently after the old mill owner left for America because of a bad speculation he had made, causing him to lose his mill there in Milton. Wilson was a newcomer to the town of Milton and was learning the rules and regulations of the cotton trade.

John hadn't told Margaret much about Mr. Wilson or where he was from because John himself hadn't gotten to know him very well yet.

The carriage was getting close to the house now as they went down the last stretch of thoroughfare. There it stood, overwhelming in the shadows that it cast down on the street below. The mighty gates, looming in the shadows, were built of solid wood and could withstand quite a lot of pressure brought against them, as the workers had proven in the past. The overseer, Finn, lived to the side of the factory itself. He was a single man of considerable age who was always there to assist John in whatever needed to be done. He could be quite authoritative and had gotten angry with workers before. He had not acted wisely when dealing with the situation. John had confidence in him, though, and had put a certain amount of trust in Finn.

Margaret noticed the gates starting to open as the carriage reached it, and they pulled into the small factory yard as Finn closed the gates behind them. Finn came to the door of the carriage and opened it as John stepped out onto the step. John turned around and offered one of his hands to Margaret as she stepped out of the carriage filled with worry over how her soon-to-be mother-in-law would handle their arrival.

CHAPTER 3

The candles were burning bright in the house as Margaret looked up atthe windows. There she could see Mrs. Thornton looking down at them like a big black angry crow, ready to guard her nest and anyone daring to intrude on it. The light caused Mrs. Thornton's silhouette to look like a menacing shadow in the window. John was busy getting the bags and didn't notice. He turned to Margaret and offered his arm as he gave the bags to Sarah, one of the housemaids, to carry into the house. They walked up the stairs to the house as Finn went to take care of the horses.

Mrs. Thornton was still standing by the window when they arrived in the sitting room. "And how was your trip?" she asked calmly. "I see Margaret has come back with you." She gave Margaret a slight glance. "To discuss the mill, I presume?"

"I have good news, Mother. We are going to be able to hire back all of our workers," said John.

"Really? How did this happen?" asked Mrs. Thornton.

"Margaret is going to help with that," said John as Mrs. Thornton turned from the window with a frown.

"I wouldn't have been able to stand it if the mill had closed. I was sad at the very thought of it being all empty and abandoned," said Margaret, walking toward Mrs. Thornton. "I have some money to invest, and I think we can use it to run the mill."

Mrs. Thornton looked down from her taller height at Margaret without expression. "Well, Margaret, you must be tired. I'll have Sarah show you to a room." She called out for Sarah and instructed her to take Margaret up to a room. Margaret hesitated with a look at John and then nodded to Mrs. Thornton. After Margaret had left the room, Mrs. Thornton motioned for John to sit down. "Now tell me how this all came about," she demanded when Margaret and Sarah were out of earshot.

"As you know, I went to London to see Henry Lennox. Only when I got there, Henry was detained at some meeting. But Margaret was there. She had some papers drawn up, explaining how she could make better interest on her money if she used it to help me run Marlborough Mill. So that is what she proposed to do. She said I could think of it as a business arrangement, but before I left here, I saw Nicholas Higgins, who told me about her brother. Frederick had secretly visited here while their mother lay dying. He was the man who was at the station with her that night. I knew then that she had only been protecting him from the law," John explained, seeing his mother's expression change to one of concern. "Don't worry. I'll explain that later. To continue, when I saw Margaret and after having heard this explanation, I realized that she felt differently about me, so I asked her to marry me. I still love her, Mother, and she loves me as well, so you are looking at a very happy man."

"I still cannot believe she deserves you, but I won't stand in the way of your happiness." Despite her acquiescence, Mrs. Thornton still looked dismayed at the idea of John marrying Margaret and from the knowledge that she would now be second in his heart.

Margaret had been led to a lovely room with curtains of green velvet. Sarah hurried to turn down the bed and get some water for her to wash up. Margaret thought about how long it had been since she had last been to Milton. It seemed almost a lifetime ago, even though it had only been a year. Milton looked the same to her with its drafty old houses and smoky skies. But it was also different as well because this time she came to Milton with a new respect for the town and for the people who tried to survive here. Tomorrow she would go visit Mary and Nicholas, but she was certain to hear from Mrs. Thornton on that subject. John was coming up the hallway as Margaret peeked out of the room to see if Sarah was on her way.

"You look tired. I'm surprised you're still up," he said.

"I'm just waiting on Sarah to wash up and then I plan to go to bed," said Margaret.

"Well, I will see you in the morning then." John kissed her softly and continued down the hall to his room with a smile. He remembered suddenly that he would have to go see Higgins the next day to discuss getting the men to come back. He turned before he got to his room and faced Margaret, who had been watching him go. "I'll be gone early tomorrow morning on business, so I will leave you in my mother's care."

"I'll be fine, John." Margaret laughed at his look of concern. "I have some things to do as well." She waved at him and went back into her room.

John stood at his door for a few minutes, watching her go into the room and wishing to be with her. Then he turned and went into his as well. The next day would be busy, and he needed some rest if he was to get everything done.

Early the next morning, John barely stopped for breakfast before leaving to go see Higgins. He made his way to Francis Street and circled behind the Golden Dragon to reach the Higgins house. He knocked on the door and waited for several long minutes before the door finally opened. Mary stood in the doorway, and when she saw Mr. Thornton, she asked, "Are you, here to see Dad?"

"Yes, this is about business," said John. Nicholas was coming down the stairs putting on his shirt and stopped at the bottom of the stairs when he saw John.

"Ah, Master, what are you doing here?" asked Higgins. "Did you see Miss Margaret when you were in London?"

"Yes, I did, and in fact, she has come back with me," said Thornton, smiling.

"I thought that might happen. I knew you had a soft spot for her, and her for you," said Higgins, grinning from ear to ear.

"Yes, I'm very happy," said Thornton.

"I had a feeling if I told you about her brother, you would go looking for her," Higgins confessed.

"Well, today I've come on business. You know that list of men you gave me? I would like for them to come work for me at the mill again."

"Don't worry, Master. I'll round up the men, and we'll be there shortly," Higgins assured him as he put on his shoes. "Mary, get those kids to school! I'll see you at the mill," he said to Thornton, and they left the house. John parted ways with Higgins and made his way back to the mill to speak to the overseer about making the arrangements that needed to be made for the cotton deliveries and such.

Stepping out of the house and putting on her cover, Margaret looked up at the sky searching for any rain and then proceeded down the steps. She was just leaving as John was coming up the front stairs. "Where are you going?" asked John.

"I was going to see Nicholas," said Margaret.

"Well, he's on business for me, but maybe you will see him later," said John. "I need you to come with me for the moment." He took her arm.

"What is it?"

"I need those papers you showed me in London. In all the excitement, I forgot to sign them, and I need to get them back to Henry," said John.

"Oh, of course," she replied, heading to her room to retrieve them. John followed her but stopped at the door when they reached it. "I'll wait here while you get them. We don't want to give any of the servants something to talk about, do we?" He smiled at her. Margaret just smiled and entered the room to get the papers. She came out with them and gave them to John. "I'll sign these and get them off to Henry immediately," said John. "Now, I need to go to the mill, so I'll see you at dinner." He kissed her cheek and hand before he left.

John walked to the mill, glad to be running it again. The workers were all arriving as he made it to his office. As he was going in, he caught Stevens trying to come in. He turned and shouted, "Stevens, I'm not letting you back into my mill! Be gone with you!" Stevens appeared to ignore the shout, but was stopped short by Higgins and the overseer.

"You've made enough trouble. You need to go," said Higgins, pushing him out of the gates. He watched to make sure Stevens continued down the street.

The horses arrived with the bags of raw cotton, the offloading started, and their business sprung back to life. Half the day was gone before the mill started really working again, but they would have to work hard to catch up. The orders they had before the factory had closed would be due soon. John was happy to find out if they got the first order done on time. Since there was a new time schedule, they would be back in business, but it would certainly be a struggle. If they all worked together, they could do it.

Back at the house, Margaret went into the drawing room to find Mrs. Thornton looking out the window at the workers, standing guard as usual. John's mother turned her attention to Margaret as she walked in. "John tells me I am to give my blessing to you and him," said Mrs. Thornton coldly. "I never thought I would have to concern myself with you ever again. I guess I was mistaken."

Margaret looked at her sadly. "I guess I could have expected that reaction, especially after the way I acted toward your son. But please know this. I realized what I was giving up almost immediately after I turned him down. But it wouldn't have done any good to have told him that at the time." Attempting to change the subject, she asked, "Do you think we will have to worry about strikes anymore?"

"There will always be people out there who will not be satisfied by whatever they get," said Mrs. Thornton, frowning.

"I know that John will try his best," said Margaret.

Mrs. Thornton's turned to her in anger. "Don't worry, girl. My son won't lose your money for you, if that's what you are concerned about!"

"That is the last thing on my mind right now," said Margaret, getting irritated. "I only meant that I believe in what he does and in how hard he works to keep it going. I admire him for who he is."

John entered the house just as Margaret went to stand by the window. She couldn't believe how hard this was going to be. Mrs. Thornton wasn't going to give up control over her son very easily, and she was making that abundantly clear from the very start. Margaret comforted herself with the knowledge that John loved both her and his mother, and she would just have to make it work for his sake. John came over to the window, walking past his mother, and stood behind Margaret, putting his hands on her waist. "Doesn't it look great seeing all the workers down there?" he asked.

"It is nice to know that I am helping you with the mill," said Margaret. "I feel at last that my money is being put to good use." With a quick glance, she could see Mrs. Thornton starting to pout as she watched them at the window. Surely she felt pushed aside, as he would no longer ask her for her guidance but would turn to Margaret now.

Mrs. Thornton felt tears sting her eyes as she remembered all the times she had held her son up when he seemed to be falling, as she had told him a mother's love is everlasting. She wondered if Margaret could say the same about her feelings for him. Mrs. Thornton decided that she was going to make it her business to find out. She would test Margaret's love for her son. Mrs. Thornton was determined to find out what kind of stuff this Southern girl was made of. Time would tell if she was worthy of him and if she needed to get John away from Ms. Margaret Hale before he lost all sense of himself.

CHAPTER 4

John was checking the shipments and bulks of cotton when Inspector Mason walked up to him. "Sir, it has been brought to the attention of our department that Mr. Silas Slickson may be abusing some of his workers. Children, to be exact. It has been rumored that Mr. Slickson has been chaining some of the children to the machinery in his factory. Also, it was told to the department that he is working some of the children over twelve hours a day with no break for a meal. Because you are the magistrate of Milton, I must request that you come with me to Mr. Slickson's to check out the charges, sir."

John called to Finn and left instructions for the workers that day and how much was to be done in the sorting rooms. He led the inspector to the factory yard. Williams, who had previously been the overseer for John, had gone to Mr. Slickson after John had fired him for severely beating some workers, and Mr. Slickson had made Williams his overseer. John walked into the yard to see Williams beating a young boy of sixteen years who hadn't been loading the cotton to Williams's satisfaction. John glared and made his way into the mill. The floors were unsanitary, and white fluffs of cotton were blowing around in the air. Some of the workers looked ill and were still on the job. "He shouldn't have those workers here in that condition. He won't make his orders," he told Mason. John saw Silas on the floor, yelling at a woman to either finish the weaving or he would fine her for unsatisfactory work. Silas turned to find John standing there. Mason saw evidence of chains and leg cuffs near some of the spinning looms. A little girl named Victoria came up to them and started picking up cotton at their feet. John looked down at her. She looked about six or seven and had bruises and marks on her ankles. John stepped over her as it dawned on him he had seen her before. She was the same little girl he had given money to on Francis Street while going to see Higgins. John's face clouded with anger as he grabbed Silas by his collar and yelled at him, "What do you think you are doing? You do this to your workers and we all have to suffer for it!" He shoved Silas backward into some cotton and then turned and started to walk back out of the mill. Silas came up from behind him and grabbed him by the shoulder, swinging John around and socking him in the jaw. John drew back to hit him with his fist, anger glaring from his eyes, when his senses returned to him. He blocked Silas's hits and yelled, "Stop it! We need to deal with this like grown men! Mason has told me that you have been accused of mistreating your workers, and they want to press charges against you." The man stop swinging. "So what do you have to say to these charges?"

Silas said, "I won't admit to any of the charges. I haven't been mistreating my workers! It is all a pack of lies!" John stared at him in disbelief since he had seen the little girl's marks and had witnessed the overseer, Williams, beating the boy.

"If I come back here and see any signs of children being chained to machines or your overseer thrashing a worker, I will press charges myself! You are putting all our mills in jeopardy with your tomfoolery. Do you understand?" John turned and walked out of the mill, opening and closing his fists as he thought about Slickson and his stupidity.

Mason followed him out into the yard. "That's not exactly the way I was thinking of handling it by seeing you two fighting." Mason looked at him, surprised. "Do you think that did any good? Displaying that kind of behavior in front of the workers? You might have caused more riots against the masters now. I will leave this for you to handle for now, but I will have to file a report on what I saw and witnessed. I think it would be a good idea to have a meeting with all the masters. Maybe something can be done."

"I will get back to you by Thursday next," said John, leaving Mason and heading back to Marlborough Mill.

Months later, a law was passed requiring children under nine not to be used in the mills at all for gathering cotton pieces. Most local magistrates didn't enforce the law, though. Only John had considered enforcing it.

John came into the house that evening and said he had quite a few workers from other mills coming to talk to him about working at Marlborough Mill. "They all seem to have the same complaint. They don't like the working conditions at the mills where they work," he told Margaret.

"Maybe when I have the meeting with the other masters, something can be done about it. I would rather the workers stay where they are, and then I can find a way of improving their conditions."

"Is it really worse than it was before?" Margaret asked, watching him walk to the window.

"I don't know if it's that or if it's because they know they can ask for more now with the laws changing for their benefit. Or at least that's what they think," said John.

"I know you'll think of something, John. You wouldn't let them suffer unnecessarily." Margaret touched his arm as he looked out the window and down at the mill.

"I believe you have more faith in me than I do in myself," said John, looking sideways at her.

"Well, it will all work out." Margaret put her hand on his shoulder and gazed out the window and down onto the heads of the workers moving below.

The following morning, John went to see the other masters to have a meeting with them. They had the meeting in the Alexander business building on the town square. Silas, of course, arrived a little drunk, wearing a bruise on his face similar to the ones on John's jaw. Harland Henderson, Horatio Hamper, and Wilfred Wilson were already there and just stared at Silas when he arrived. "Good God, man! What are you thinking coming in here to a meeting all drunk and stumbling?" asked Harland, totally taken aback by Silas's condition.

John got their attention by saying, "I have called you all here to discuss the treatment of the workers in our factories. Apparently, Silas here," he pointed to Silas, "has been chaining some of the children in his factory to machines. These reports have gotten to the inspectors, and I have been called in as magistrate to try to sort it all out." The other masters looked at Silas.

"These reports I suppose were put in by workers?" asked Horatio. "I think we should find out who they are and have them strapped and fined. That would put an end to it."

John looked at Horatio and said, "Beating the workers is the reason we are all in this predicament right now." Looking over at Silas, he said, "Silas you are going to have to fire Williams as your overseer. He beat workers at my mill, and he now continues it at your mill. The inspector and I both saw him beating a boy when we were there yesterday. Cut him loose before he brings you down with him. Furthermore, there is to be no more chaining of children in any of the mills. It is rather barbaric, don't you think? They help us with our businesses. We don't need them complaining and possibly striking again. It would do none of us any good."

Harland looked at John. "If the workers complain and we get shut down, where will our profits go? There wouldn't be any profit in that at all."

"What we need is a way to minimize the workers' complaints and be more reasonable to their needs," said Wilfred.

"As long as it doesn't affect our profits," said Harland, grimacing.

"I have a meeting with the inspector on Thursday. We need to have solid plans for improvements in our factories," said John. "Silas, get rid of the chains and leg cuffs. You shouldn't have had them in the first place.

"I know I wouldn't have them in my mill," said Harland. "Get rid of Williams, like John advised. He'll have to leave and that will be good for the town. It will be far less trouble for everyone, even if it costs you a little for his union compensations. At least he will be gone and away from us all. That will solve one of the problems."

"Well, it seems that Silas needs to do some adjusting at his factory so the rest of us don't suffer," said Wilfred.

"We all will have to make sure that the workers don't get any other reasons to complain. With the constant threats of strikes, we need to try to not upset them any more than they already are," said John. "I think you all need to have a meeting with your workers just to smooth things over because believe me, I'm sure they all know about the complaints filed by now with the inspectors. Be on your guard, all of you. This could be an explosive situation if not handled right. A newspaper recently wrote that the cotton mills are becoming places of sexual license, foul language, cruelty, violent accidents, and alien manners, and that the mills show harsh punishments, unhealthy working conditions, low wages, and inflexible, long working hours. Some of these can't be avoided if we are to make a profit, but with things like this being written in the newspaper and the inspectors starting to watch us more closely, we have to be careful how we handle matters at hand. I see a lot more fines and possible imprisonment for anyone not acting more responsible with their business affairs."

"We need to go evaluate our workers and overseers and see that they are getting the jobs done appropriately," said Harland. "It will come back on us if they are not following our instructions."

John motioned that the meeting was over. Harland, Wilfred, and Horatio all grabbed their hats and started for the door.

John turned to Silas and asked him to stay behind a moment. "You know what you have to do, so make sure you do it," said John as he handed Silas his hat and followed him out of the meeting hall, closing the door to the hall behind him. John shook his head as he watched Silas leave down the street.

John made his way down the streets to the mill. He was deep in thought as he made his way across the yard to the house. He needed a stiff drink to sort his mind and calm his nerves. Mrs. Thornton was standing at her customary spot looking out the window and down onto the yard. John entered the room to find that Margaret had gone to visit with Fanny for a while and that Mrs. Thornton had been watching the workers.

"John, how did the meeting go?"

"As good as could be expected. It is all up to the other masters now. They need to straighten it all out at their own factories. I will meet with Mason on Thursday and tell him it has been taken care of, and I believe after meeting with the other masters, I will suggest that they fine Silas Slickson. He must be made an example of this time. Mother, I'm going to have a drink and then go see Fanny and bring Margaret back. Can you watch the mill for me?"

"Of course. Go do what you need to," said Mrs. Thornton.

Later that evening, Fanny and Watson came to dinner. Fanny was all excited about the latest fashions in London. They had just returned home from there, and she was going on about the fashions to Margaret and Mrs. Thornton. "They have the nicest silks there. They really lift the spirits and are so soft. I guess you'll know all about that, wouldn't you, Margaret?"

Margaret nodded, but she was more interested in what the men were discussing about the mills. Wilson had hired Stevens on at his mill. John was saying he hoped that Stevens wouldn't burn anything down considering he couldn't be trusted not to smoke and what a fool Wilson was for hiring him. He also related the business with Silas Slickson to Watson. "Having that meeting was the best thing you could have done at this point. You're quite right," said Watson.

Fanny had barely noticed that Margaret wasn't listening to her, but Mrs. Thornton noticed and told Fanny to talk of something else. Fanny got a big smile on her face as she told Margaret and Mrs. Thornton she had just found out she was pregnant. Finally, she had gotten everyone's attention. Margaret, Mrs. Thornton, and John all turned to look at her.

"Fanny, when did you find this out?" asked Mrs. Thornton. "We found out on the trip to London," said Fanny.

"Oh my goodness. Congratulations!" said Margaret, smiling.

Thinking about how she sometimes reacted to things, John asked her, "Are you ready to be a mother, Fanny?"

"Of course I am," said Fanny, frowning at him. Margaret just looked at him and smiled.

Mrs. Thornton had been thinking the same thing but wasn't going to voice it. "I'll be here if Fanny needs anything," said Mrs. Thornton, smiling at her daughter.

"I knew she could count on you, Mother," said John, smiling at her.

Mrs. Thornton smiled at John and said, "You'll be fine, Fanny. We're all here for you. Don't worry. You won't have a care."

CHAPTER 5

A month had passed. Margaret started making plans for the wedding. Fanny was always handy, giving advice and suggestions. Margaret thought about what she had once said to Henry about walking to church on a summer's day for her wedding and decided that maybe it was not a reasonable thing to consider. They were living in Milton, after all, where there was always smoke in the air. Her dress would be ruined if she walked all the way to the church in it. She could have some flowers in the church and wouldn't have to have any ridiculous baubles in her hair. The dress she choose was simple in its design but was made of silk and lace with embroidered flowers.

Unknown to Margaret, John was going to Helstone to get the yellow flowers she loved so much to put in her bouquet. He was claiming a trip for business as a ruse so she wouldn't know. Edith, Mrs. Shaw, and Captain Lennox were coming to the wedding and would be arriving at the end of the week. Sarah had been busy getting all the extra rooms ready. Mrs. Shaw had written to say she would take care of the flowers, and that it was the least she could do for her niece. Mary had stopped by to say that she and Nicholas would be there. Mrs. Thornton had thought it was wrong to have them at the wedding, but John had told her it was what Margaret wanted and he wanted her to be happy. Fanny was having fainting spells, probably due to the heat, so Dr. Donaldson had advised her to stay in bed and rest unless she didn't want to go to the wedding in a week's time. Mrs. Thornton promised to make her obey and to visit her each day. Margaret started taking her walks again and would even go into the mill with John to watch the workers. It brought back memories of him standing on the top steps the first time she came into the factory. How proud he had looked. She started helping with the workers' evening meals, assisting Mary. Sometimes Nicholas started making lists for the food and gave them to Margaret so she could go with Mary to purchase it. Margaret wanted to make sure the butcher was giving them a fair price. John dealt with most of the figures, but

Margaret wanted to keep an eye on the business as well. At first, John didn't like it too well, but Margaret told him she was interested in all aspects of the trade industry and wouldn't be discouraged. Finally, John let her help with certain things concerning the mill, just as his mother had. It had also given Margaret an opportunity to help out and learn about the business in the process. She learned to care for its ins and outs of the daily schedule as much as John always did.

Margaret was going into the drapery shop when she saw Ann Latimer coming up the walk. "Oh, Ann, how have you been?"

"I'm doing fine," said Ann, looking down her nose at Margaret. "I understand you are marrying Mr. Thornton."

"Yes, we are to marry this weekend." Margaret noticed that Ann looked a little dismayed at the news.

"Well, Father and I will be there. After all, it is a society thing."

"I really don't care for some society," said Margaret, lifting her chin a little higher as she remembered how Ann had always clung to John's arm when they spent time together several years ago.

"Good day, Margaret," said Ann coldly, when she noticed Margaret's look of superiority.

Margaret followed her with her eyes as she continued down the walk. Ann was dismayed at the news. That was certain by her cold manner. But Margaret felt happy inside as she realized she wouldn't have to endure watching Ann put her arm into John's ever again. Margaret turned and walked into the shop. She spotted some lace on a rack in the back of the store and went over to it.

"Hi, miss. Can I help you?" Mrs. Brown asked from behind the counter. "I was admiring this lace. It is so delicate," said Margaret.

"Yes, it's the finest around," said Mrs. Brown.

"Well, I would like to buy some. Here is the money," said Margaret, handing it to her. Mrs. Brown wrapped it in brown paper and handed the lace to Margaret. The doorbell tinkled several times as she left the shop and walked back into the side street.

Margaret saw three of the Boucher children, Thomas, Emma, and Jenny, heading to Francis Street. She rushed to catch up with them. "How are the three of you doing?" asked Margaret. "I hate school," said Jenny.

"I like school all right, but I don't want to work in the mills someday," said Emma.

"Well, I plan to be a master someday, so I need all this learning," said Thomas, smiling up at her.

"Well, with hard work I'm sure you can do anything," said Margaret, giving Thomas a wink.

"Well, we have to go, miss. We're helping Mary with the food tonight," said Jenny. They walked on, and Margaret continued to the mill.

Those children were lucky to be with Nicholas and Mary, thought Margaret. Since their parents had died and Nicholas had taken them in, the children had felt rather lost in the world of industry. The other children of the Boucher's were Lizzie, Simon, Frank, Karl, and Marc. They were living in five other homes among other workers, and Margaret wasn't sure their fate would be as good. The poverty that surrounded so many of the workers made it hard for anyone to take in an orphaned child.

She crossed the yard to the house and went inside, hanging up her bonnet and going down the hallway. Coming into the sitting room she walked to the table where she had ideas for the wedding laid out. Looking up, she noticed John at the window looking down into the yard. "I want to talk to you about the wedding," said Margaret, looking down at the papers on the table.

John walked to the table to look. "Don't forget that I will be leaving for a meeting on Thursday and probably won't be back until the day of the wedding."

"Don't worry. I haven't forgotten," Margaret said, looking down at the list she had. "What do you think would be best for the dinner after the wedding?"

"Whatever you want will be fine with me," said John. Suddenly feeling regretful, he said, "I'm so sorry we won't be able to go away right away for a holiday together."

"We are going to the lodgings at the edge of town for a day or two together alone," said Margaret, looking up at him. "That's more than I could have dreamed of at a time like this."

John didn't know if he could possibly love her anymore then he did right now, but her comment only made him cherish her more.

"Don't worry. We'll have lots of opportunities in the future to go on holiday," said Margaret, smiling at him. His eyes were twinkling with the thoughts of the wedding to come and the way she would look when she walked down the aisle toward him on their wedding day. Those thoughts would get him through the next few days.

Mrs. Shaw, Captain Lennox, and Edith arrived two days before the wedding, just as John was leaving to go to his meeting out of town. Margaret was kissing him good-bye when they pulled up. "Good-bye. I will see you on our wedding day," said Margaret as he pulled away. He nodded to the Captain and then was gone.

"Oh, Margaret, I didn't realize how very smoky it is here," said Edith, alarmed for the boy's health.

"I've gotten used to it, and besides, it is really not as bad as it seems," said Margaret.

"Where is John off to?" asked Captain Lennox.

"He has a business meeting out of town," said Margaret as Mrs. Shaw looked at Edith and smiled. John had written to find out if she would object to him getting flowers from Helstone for the wedding. Of course she had thought it a splendid idea and had written back to tell him so. Sarah and Finn came up to help with the bags and horses and such. Mrs. Shaw put her arm in Margaret's as she inquired about Mrs. Thornton and everyone.

"Hannah is with Fanny, who is pregnant and on bed rest until the wedding. Orders came straight from Dr. Donaldson. He wouldn't let her refuse. We can go see her later," said Margaret.

"I have written to Frederick and told him about the wedding. He was surprised to hear of it but sent his best wishes. I just wish Henry would have found a way to help him so he could have been here and I could have met Delores finally," said Margaret.

"Frederick would like your Mr. Thornton, I think," said Mrs. Shaw, turning to smile at Margaret and kiss her cheeks.

Meanwhile at Fanny's, Fanny was sitting in a silk night dress when they arrived to visit her. Mrs. Thornton had gone to order some tea to be brought up, and Fanny just sparkled when she realized everyone had come to visit her. "My dear, how are you feeling? Margaret has told us everything," said Mrs. Shaw.

"Well, I am so delicate, but the doctor says I should be fine after I rest." Mrs. Thornton came in as Edith was asking about her fine linens. "They are imported. John would disapprove because it is not from his factory, but I think they are quite fine." Emily, Fanny's maid, came in with the tea and sat it down on the cabinet. She proceeded to pour everyone a cup and then left the room. Mrs. Shaw took a seat near the window as Fanny went on about her delicate condition and how this pregnancy was draining her so.

"I'm sure the rest will do wonders," said Edith, hoping she had never appeared that delicate to others.

Mrs. Thornton looked at Mrs. Shaw and asked her what she thought of Milton's fine businesses. "I haven't seen much of them, but the streets do seem a bit dusty, don't they?" asked Mrs. Shaw.

Mrs. Thornton moved in her chair uncomfortably as she replied, "The streets do get a bit dusty, but that is to be expected with the coal from the factories always burning up into the air. Although after awhile you hardly seem to notice it."

Mrs. Shaw tried to make light of it, but it was apparent that she couldn't stand to be there and was showing her disdain for all to witness. Margaret tried to change the subject by referring to quality goods that could be purchased in Milton. It seemed to give Mrs. Shaw the out to no longer concentrate on the town or the people. Mrs. Thornton looked at Margaret and was slightly impressed with the way she had handled the situation. Maybe there was hope yet that Margaret wasn't as bad as Mrs. Thornton thought. But she would still be watching her, looking for anything that might hurt her son or cause him pain or displeasure.

On the day of the wedding, the time was fast approaching and Margaret hadn't gotten any word that John had returned. She started to pace as she considered if something had happened to him. It would mean her world had once again crumbled around her, and this was one blow she was afraid she wouldn't survive. Edith entered to see her and stopped in the doorway when she saw her cousin standing before her in a beautiful layered white silk dress trimmed with lace, pearls, and crystals with lace sleeves. The white veil with tiny pearls scattered through the lace hung about her face, causing a beautiful illusion around her features. Slender white lace gloves adorned her hands, which she would take off before the ceremony and then wear again when they were married. Upon closer inspection, she noticed a tear on Margaret's cheek.

"Margaret, what's wrong? Are you scared?" asked Edith.

"No! It's not anything like that. I just haven't heard from John yet, and I'm just worried, that's all."

Edith went to hug her cousin. "John will be here! Don't worry so. You need to look your best today, and you don't want him to think he caused you any worry, do you?"

"No, of course not," said Margaret. She went to her bedroom window and looked out onto the street. Finn was down below getting the horses ready. Just then, another horse and carriage pulled into the yard. She saw Finn remove his hat and and make a bow. He started talking to whoever was in the buggy. Captain Lennox stepped from the carriage and then she saw John stepping out. She sighed with relief. She had been holding her breath and hadn't even realized it until now. Edith, seeing her intake of breath, came to the window to look.

"See? I told you he'd be fine," said Edith cheerfully. "Come now. We need to get you to the church." Margaret smiled at her cousin as they made their way to the horses outside. John had gone into the mill to do something, so Margaret was able to leave without him seeing her in her gown and veil. The horses made their way to the church, and Margaret stepped out. Mrs. Thornton, Mrs. Shaw, and the boys had followed them in another carriage. Behind them had been Watson and John. Edith came around to help her cousin as they made their way to the room where Margaret was supposed to wait for the service to begin. Margaret caught a glimpse of the church. It had yellow roses from Helstone everywhere along the seats. Margaret gasped as she looked at them. Edith came up to her and said, "That's where John went. He wanted it to be perfect for you."

"You mean he didn't have a meeting?" Margaret asked, looking in awe at the flowers.

"No, he didn't," Edith said, smiling.

They walked to the room and waited. Upon hearing the music,

they proceeded into the church's sanctuary, walking to the rhythm of the music and stepping slowly. The church was full of people. John's business acquaintances, friends of both John and her, Mrs. Shaw, Captain Lennox, Edith, the boys, Mrs. Thornton, Fanny, and Watson were all sitting in the front of the church. As the music started, she saw John walk in with the priest. He turned to face her as she made her way up the aisle. John's eyes shone with appreciation as he looked at her. The dress made her look like the most beautiful person he had ever put his eyes upon. He smiled and took her hand. Margaret looked up at John. He looked dashing in his top hat and suit. She listened to the words of commitment she was making to John, and at that moment, she realized that she felt as if they were all alone standing up there making a pledge to honor each other in all that they did from that point forward. She felt her heart would burst and glanced at John as he put her ring on her finger. She loved every hair on his head and would stand between him and any danger just like she had once before. John then looked at her and said, "You belong to me now, and I will never let you go." He bent his head and kissed her tenderly on the lips as everyone cheered and yelled their celebrations.John and Margaret made their way back down the aisle and through the people outside to get into their carriage. John laughed as ribbons and confetti got stuck in the ribbon on his top hat. "You are completely covered with confetti," he told Margaret as they climbed into the carriage and Margaret started taking pieces out of her hair and veil. John reached up and started to take his hat off, which caused ribbons and confetti to fall down over his face.

Margaret looked at him and started laughing. "You put on quite the show," she teased him.

"I love to hear you happy," said John, smiling and watching as she wiped the confetti off his shirt. Taking the carriage back to the house, they had their dinner reception and then said their good-byes to their friends and family as once again they were on their way in the carriage to their weekend getaway.

"The lodging is just up here," said John, pointing through the window of the carriage. "We should be quite cozy tonight," he added with a twinkle in his eye. Margaret blushed and looked out the window into the meadows. She never thought she would ever marry. The probability of it had always seemed so remote to her. She was happy to have been wrong. She couldn't think of anywhere she would rather be than sitting beside this man who had just became her husband and friend for life. They would have a great life. She just knew it. After all, they had been through so much to get to this point in their relationship, and now they would always be together and have each other to lean on in the hard and desperate times ahead.

CHAPTER 6

The carriage pulled up to an old house that was on the edge of Milton. From the outside, it looked kind of out of place, at least in the sense that it almost looked as if it belonged in the countryside somewhere. The man who owned and lent it out came walking down the path to help with their bags. They hadn't brought a lot since they were only going to be there a few days. Mrs. Thornton had said she would run the day-to-day operations of the mill so they could at least have this short time together. There was a small porch on the back of the house that overlooked some meadows. It was almost sundown by the time they arrived, and the early evening view was nice. There was still some of the smoke of Milton bearing down on this area, but one could see the sky more clearly here. John put his hands on her shoulders as she leaned back against him and they both watched as the sun went down behind the line of trees, which was to the West.

Margaret turned around and put her arms around his waist. Looking up at him, she asked, "So, Mr. Thornton, what shall we have to eat?"

John, distracted by how close she was, cleared his throat and said, "What do you want, Mrs. Thornton?" It came out like a whisper.

Margaret smiled and said, "All I really want is you." John bent his head and kissed her softly on her cheeks and then her lips, with true longing for what was to come. Then he took her hand and led her into the house.

When the first slivers of light shone through the window the next morning, Margaret was lying in his arms and looking up at his face as he slept soundly beside her. He had such perfect English lines to his face. His nose was long and slender but perfect for his face. His dark hair was caressing the lines of his forehead, and for the first time, she noticed a small indentation on his forehead. She slowly moved her hand up and put a finger on the spot to touch it. John stirred, opened his eyes, and reached up and took her hand in his and kissed it. "I got that when I was a boy. I fell into a river by my school and almost drowned. I'm sorry to say that I fear water a little now because of it."

"I think all men have fears. They have fears of the heart, they fear for their soul, and fear for those they care for," said Margaret, smiling. "It is nothing to be ashamed of. I think my only fear would be of failing in your eyes." She kissed him on the nose as she started to get out of bed.

"What makes you think I want you to get up?" asked John. "Well, we can't just lie here all day, can we?" she teased.

"I think I could very easily, yes," said John, smiling, putting his arms under his head.

"What sense would there be in that when the day is so beautiful and the meadows are calling to us?" Margaret laughed at him.

"Very well then. We shall take a picnic to the meadow," said John, groaning as he rolled out of bed.

Seeing his bare back as he rose from the bed, Margaret realized she had forgotten about her state of undress and pulled the covers quickly over herself. John had his back to her as he put on his pants and laughed when he heard the rustle of the covers on the bed. "It's too late, my dear. I have seen everything." John turned around. Margaret blushed as he came and lifted her face to look at him. "You have nothing to fear from me, for I adore you." He gave her body a final glance.

Margaret dressed as he went to get the owner to prepare them a picnic of chicken, fruit, and salad. He also had to get the carriage ready for the short trip to the far side of the meadow where there was a little clearing with a babbling brook. As they approached it, it looked green and soft with lots of flowers, and the birds were singing. The meadows smelled fragrant and sweet. Margaret found a spot by the brook on the edge of some trees that looked inviting and put down a covering on the ground. The owner had prepared a meal of chicken and small cakes with tea to drink and salad and fruit as well. Margaret laid out the food as John opened each package to look at what had been packed. Margaret had never really enjoyed picnics in London, but here in the North it was more relaxed and calm with all its open spaces. Margaret noticed a bird that came to drink from the brook.

It was kind of small and had hardly any feathers on its wings. "Look, John!" She pointed at the bird. "The poor little thing. It suffers as much as the people do."

"You will find that life can be hard for everyone and everything at times here in the North," said John. "You only have seen some of the trials that go on here, but I can tell you there are a lot more things to suffer around Milton and other places as well." He took out his watch to see the time, and Margaret remarked on seeing it always with him. "Yes, it was my father's. I keep it to remind me of where I come from and where I want to go."

"It looks very unique compared to watches I have seen in the past," said Margaret.

"My father had it specially made. He had just received it from the clockmaker a few weeks before he died." John's eyes clouded with the memory. He handed the watch to Margaret. It was antique gold with a carving of his family crest on the front. As Margaret opened it, she noticed a little carved bird inside the lid. Under the bird was written, "Always soar like a bird." The face of the watch was white with black Roman numerals and had fancy scalloped hands. It was a handsome piece of jewelry. It was understandable why John took great pride in wearing it.

"Well, I guess you will just have to pass it to your son someday," said Margaret, smiling as she handed it back to John.

He hooked it back onto his pocket and glanced up at Margaret, noticing the light reflecting off her hair and thinking it looked like shiny chestnuts. Margaret, lost in thoughts of her parents, glanced into the water, not really seeing anything. John suspected her thoughts and told her he thought her parents would have been glad to see her so happy at last and to see her starting a life of her own with John, who her father had liked.

Those two days away from everyday life had worked its magic as they returned to the house at Marlborough Mill. They were unaware that Mrs. Thornton had been watching for them through the window. It would take some time for her to get used to Margaret being first in John's life. Hannah met their happy faces as they walked in.

"It's lovely to see you both so happy," said Mrs. Thornton, hugging them both as she instructed a servant to take their bags up to their new room. She had put together the room while they were gone. She had put up new wallpaper and artwork and had given the room new furniture as well.

CHAPTER 7

A month had come and gone. Where has the time gone? Margaret thought as she decided that she wanted to make an outfit for Fanny's baby. She would go to Brown's drapery shop for the lace she had gotten for her wedding. She loved that lace, and it would look perfect to trim the outfit with. She headed out the front door just as John was coming in for some tea. He asked her where she was off to and then went into the house. The mill yard was buzzing with workers as she made her way through them to the gate and then the street. She walked down the sidewalk to Brown's shop. Margaret had just entered when Mrs. Brown started telling her about the loss to their business. "Have you heard? It was in the papers today. A whole shipment of delicate lace was stolen from Outwood Station right off the train!" said Mrs. Brown. "It's the same exact kind that you bought for your wedding not too long ago."

"Oh, and I had admired that lace. It was quite fine looking and, as you said, very delicate," said Margaret. "Is the robbery going to affect your shop?

"I'm afraid so. Part of that shipment was for our shop, and the other part was for Baxter's store," said Mrs. Brown, handing Margaret some other laces they carried. "Those might work for your next project." Mrs. Brown apologized for not having some of the other lace for her.

"Well, it can't be helped. Hopefully, they will catch the thieves and you will get your lace back," said Margaret, noticing Mrs. Brown's downtrodden face.

"The inspector was here earlier and said they have some leads. But that was all he would say," said Mrs. Brown.

"I'm sure the inspector will do his best," said Margaret, deciding on some light-beige lace. Mrs. Brown carefully laid the lace in some brown paper and wrapped it.

"Come back and see me again," said Mrs. Brown as Margaret headed for the shop door.

"You can count on it," said Margaret. "I never tire of making things that will impress my mother-in-law with my skills." Margaret smiled as she left. She decided that since she was so close, she would walk to Nicholas's home to visit Mary for a while. As she was walking, she saw Elizabeth walking toward her. Elizabeth was a neighbor of Nicholas's who worked at

Wilson's mill along with her husband and three of her children.

"How are you doing, Mrs. Thornton?" Elizabeth asked as she came to stand with Margaret.

"I'm doing well. How are you?" Margaret was still getting used to be called Mrs. Thornton.

"I'm fine, but my husband, Andrew, is sick with the congestion in his lungs."

"Has his lungs gotten really bad yet?" Margaret asked

"It's not too bad, but it's to be expected working in the mills and all," said Elizabeth. "He's been sick for about six weeks now, so we've been feeling the strain a bit. Losing the pound and shillings per week has really put a strain on us all."

"Is there any way I can help out?" Margaret asked, handing her some money.

"No, Mrs. Thornton. I can't take that," said Elizabeth, looking dismayed. "It's for the children," said Margaret, trying to convince her to take it. "We'll do all right. Thanks for offering anyway." Elizabeth handed the

money back. "I've been selling things for money so I can hang on until Andrew is back to work." Elizabeth said good-bye and continued on her way home.

Margaret headed for Nicholas's home and knocked on the door. Mary answered just as Margaret was about to knock again. "Hi, Mary. I thought I would come for a visit."

"Well, come in. Father isn't back yet. He's at the Golden Dragon having a pint," said Mary. Thomas and the other children were playing on the stairs when Margaret walked into the house. She went to the table and sat down. She hadn't brought food this time, as she had been preoccupied with thoughts of Fanny's baby. Mary poured her a cup of tea as Margaret watched the children on the stairs.

"How are Thomas and the others doing in school?" asked Margaret. "Thomas is becoming quite a reader," Mary said, looking over at him.

"He's going to be a smart one." They continued talking for a while when Margaret realized it was starting to get late. It was close to time for dinner, and she needed to head back home. She stood up to leave just as Nicholas arrived.

"Oh, Mrs. Margaret! I'm sorry I wasn't here to visit with you," said Nicholas.

"I will see you soon, Nicholas. We can talk then," said Margaret as she picked up her hat and started down the steps. Turning, she waved good-bye and headed back down the narrow alley path.

"I really like her. She is a fine lady," said Nicholas as he closed the door after Margaret stepped outside the house. "There are not many ladies as kind as she has been." He went to sit down at the table. Mary brought him some tea and then sat to join him. Looking at Mary, Nicholas said, "All right, Mary. We need to talk. I have heard that you have been seen talking to Mr. Henderson, the master of another mill here in town. Does he want you to come to work for him?"

"No. We have just talked a little," said Mary.

"What could you possibly have to talk about?" Nicholas looked at her, searchingly.

"Nothing really. Just general politeness, is all." Mary tried to avoid looking at Nicholas as she got up to place some biscuits on the table with some jelly. Nicholas caught her wrist as she started to walk away again and turned her around to face him.

"What is going on?" asked Nicholas.

"I'm not sure what you mean, Father. I just have talked to him. That is all." Mary glanced down at him and then looked away again.

"He is a master, Mary. Above you in stature and society. You can't cross those lines. It could turn out badly for both of us if you even entertain such thoughts." Nicholas shook his head sadly. "Mary, they don't know the suffering that we do, and most of all, they don't care to know." Finally, Mary looked straight at him. Then he said, "If you have any thoughts at all for this man, you must forget them at once. You hear me? It will never work between you two." Nicholas released her hands.

"I understand what you are saying, Father. I won't talk to him again," said Mary quietly as she started clearing the table and putting the dishes in the sink. She stood with her back to him, wiping her hands on her apron while holding back the tears that were beginning to form in her eyes. Mary understood what her father was saying, but she also knew what her heart was saying. She was falling in love with Harland. She knew socially it was wrong, and she wasn't sure how Harland felt about her. But hopefully she would know soon.

They had talked on only three occasions. The first time had been when he had seen her coming out of Marlborough Mills and he had just finished a meeting with Mr. Thornton. She had been walking across the mill yard and out the gate when he had caught up to her in his carriage and instructed his driver to take the carriage back to his house. He told the driver he wanted to take a walk and would be to the house shortly. After the carriage had left, he had walked over to Mary an asked, "Miss, do you mind if I ask you a few questions?" Mary had been a little frightened of him at first; he was tall and dark-featured, making his appearance rather overbearing. "I'm sorry, miss. I don't mean to alarm you," said Harland after seeing the look on her face.

Mary studied his face for a moment. After determining that he appeared to be nice enough, she replied, "All right. What do you want to know?"

"I was wondering exactly what it is that you do at Marlborough Mills?

Are you a servant in their house?"

"No. I am a weaver in the mill," said Mary.

"Oh, I see." Harland frowned a little as he started thinking. "Is that all you wanted to know?"

"Yes, it was." He paused and then added, "Oh no. I wanted to know your name."

"I'm Mary Higgins."

Looking surprised, Harland asked, "Did your father use to work for Horatio Hamper?"

"Yes, he did. But he now works at Marlborough Mills."

"Yes, yes, I see," said Harland, now deep in thought. "Well, Mary, it was nice talking to you." He bowed and then continued down the sidewalk. Mary stood watching him, wondering what all that had been about. Puzzled, she continued on her way home to make dinner before her father arrived home.

The second time Mary had seen Harland was when she went to Margaret's. Harland had been there on some business with Mr. Thornton, and she had been visiting with Margaret when both of the men walked into the sitting room to get some papers. Mary had looked up as Harland had entered and couldn't seem to keep her eyes off his, which were a very intense brown with golden streaks, something Mary had never seen in others' eyes. Harland, on the other hand, had been just as disturbed seeing her there. He was trying to catch what Mr. Thornton was saying to him and had glanced sideways at Mary, only to catch her staring back at him. Clearing his throat, he told Mr. Thornton that he would have to get back to him on the matter, and then with a clumsy bow to both ladies, he had left the house. Mary, having finished everything she had come to discuss with Margaret, had also made her exit, secretly hoping he would still be outside.

Mr. Henderson was just getting into his carriage when he noticed Mary coming out of the house. As he was stepping into the carriage, he asked if she would accept a ride to her street. Mary found that her voice had gotten caught in her throat and so just nodded. She climbed into the carriage and felt very drawn to him but was also a little frightened, so she just looked at him as he stared at her from across the seat.

"Well, Mary. You look very fine today," said Mr. Henderson

"Thank you." Mary blushed and looked down at her clothes. They were worn, tattered, and faded from many cleanings. How could he find my old clothes fine at all? she thought.

"I know that we don't know each other, but I would like to get to know you better," said Mr. Henderson.

Mary looked up at him and said, "I would like that too. But this could cause us some problems, though, don't you think?"

Nodding, Mr. Henderson said, "I think I can handle it," smiling at her. "How would you like to come over to my place? The servants have the day off, and I think we could get to know each other a little better there." Mary looked at him hesitantly and then agreed. She felt butterflies as she looked into those eyes she could get lost in.

They spent the entire afternoon talking and laughing. He then instructed her to call him Harland from that point on. Mary noticed the time on the street tower clock and left for home before anyone would suspect anything. But she didn't realize that she had been seen leaving his house by several people who were walking along the street.

The last time they had seen each other had only been two days earlier at the mill. He was there on business again. During their break, he asked her to come with him to his home. They had arrived just as one of the servants was leaving the house. Harland nodded to the servant and then asked Mary to follow him. Harland then turned to her, and before she realized what was happening, he was leading her to the bedroom. She tried to remain in control, but lost her will to fight it. He started kissing her, and before long, they were lying side by side and she was no longer a girl but a woman. Thinking about it now, Mary had never been happier. Harland was the man she had always dreamed about: rich, kind, handsome, and tall. What more could she ever want or need? Hadn't he showed her how much he truly cared by the way he had treated her? As though in a fog, she heard talking in the background. Mary then realized that Nicholas was still talking to her, pulling her out of her thoughts and back to reality. "I don't want you hurt," Nicholas was saying as she looked down into the sink and washed up the last dishes.

"I know, Father." Mary turned around and faintly smiled." Please don't worry, Father. I will be fine." Mary was still thinking about Harland and how he looked at her. Once again, she felt butterflies and was happy about it.

CHAPTER 8

Mason the inspector had been going through some of the evidence for the lace robbery when he came across a note from one of the people at the station. A young woman had been quoted as saying she had noticed three men near the train on the day of the robbery and they had looked rather out of place. They had appeared to be workers, and one had been overheard by the woman saying something about Henderson's mill, which was not one of the places affected by the robbery. But Mason thought it was worth checking out considering the men had mentioned it. Mason called to Inspector Riley and asked him to go with him to Harland Henderson's mill to look into the matter. Harland was busy talking to his overseer when Mason and Riley arrived.

"Can I help you?" asked Harland as he looked up and saw the inspectors. "Yes, sir. I'm Mason, and this is Riley. We are here because of the

investigation we are doing on the lace robbery at Outwood Station. It came to our attention that a woman at the station reported seeing three men who possibly work for you at the station during the time of the robbery. I was wondering, sir, if you might know who these men might be."

"The woman seemed quite positive that the three men were workers here at your mill," said Riley.

Harland thought for a moment, scratching his chin, as he thought who might have been at the station for him at the time of the robbery. "I don't remember having sent any of the men to the station at the time of the robbery, but I believe all my workers were on their break at that time."

"Well, sir, if it is all right with you, could we have the woman come here and see if she can spot the men? Then we'll know if it ties into this case or not," said Mason.

"Certainly. If any of my men are involved in this, I don't want them working for me," said Harland. Mason nodded and then stated that they would be back shortly with the woman.

Several hours later, Mason arrived with the woman. "Mr. Henderson, this is the woman who saw the men at the station." Standing in front of Harland was none other than Mary Higgins herself.

"Hello, miss. See if you can show us the men you saw at Outwood Station," said Harland, smiling at her. Mary followed the inspectors and Harland into the mill.

"All right, miss. Tell me if you can see the men who were at the station," said Mason.

Mary glanced around the room. On the far right side were all the spinning mules where most of the men worked. Just then, one of the men looked up, and when he saw the inspectors and Mary, he started running to the door of the mill. Mary shouted, "There goes one of them! He's running for the door!" Riley ran after him. Two other men started to sneak out the side of the room to go into the sorting room, but Mary saw them and pointed them out to Harland and Mason.

"Miss, you are going to be in need of protection until those three men are in jail," said Mason after he saw the look on the face of one of the men. Riley walked out to the mill yard with the captured man who had run. Harland came back with another one, but one had gotten away.

"Who are these men?" Mason asked Harland.

"This one is Andrews." Harland pointed to the one who had run. "This other one is Jacobs." He pointed at the other one. Then Harland turned to Mary and asked, "Was the other man standing next to him at the spinning mules?"

"Yes, he was right next to him," said Mary, staring at him in surprise. "Then, Inspector, the one you are looking for would be Allen. I can take

you to where he lives." Harland called to his overseer and then left with Mason, Riley, and Mary.

They had crossed the mill yard to the street when Inspector Anderson showed up to take the two men to the police station. Mason told Mary she had done well and was free to go.

"Wait, miss. It is getting dark, and it's almost time for the other workers to leave. It may not be safe for you to walk home alone without someone you know. I will get my driver to take you home." Harland held open the door and helped her into the carriage. He told the driver to take her home and then meet the inspectors at the narrow street close to where Allen lived. Mason and Riley looked at each other and then at Harland.

"I don't think anyone would be safe walking home at this hour, especially if they just ratted out fellow workers and one is still on the loose," said Harland, looking at the two inspectors.

They all climbed into the police wagon and headed to Allen's home, which was located near the lower side of the town where most of the workers lived with other families. The streets were very narrow in that part of town, and soon the inspectors and Harland had to climb out of the carriage and walk the rest of the way on foot. There was a candle shining through the window of Allen's home as they knocked on the door. After several minutes, they heard a scuffling noise coming from the back of the house. Riley went around the house to the back and found that Allen had tried to climb out the window and had gotten stuck in it. Riley whistled for Mason and Harland.

"Go bust the door down, and let's get him out of the window," said Mason. Riley kicked in the door and found children standing in the corner of the room, too terrified to move.

Meanwhile, Harland and Mason pulled on Allen's arms as Riley went over to the window and pushed on Allen, who went tumbling out the window and onto the ground below. Turning back around, Riley looked at the children, who had now been joined by their mother, and said, "Don't worry. We are only going to talk with him. It's all right. Go back to what you were doing, children." Glancing at their mother, Riley walked out of the house, shut the shambled door, and joined the others.

Mason got Allen by the shirt, pulled him up and cuffed him behind his back, and then headed off for the police station. Harland told the two inspectors that if they needed him for anything not to hesitate to call on him. With that, Harland nodded to each of the inspectors, walked back to his carriage that was waiting for him, and headed down the road to his own house.

Upon arriving at the narrow path near her home, Mary told the carriage driver that she would have to walk the rest of the way. As she got out of the carriage, everyone was staring at her. She started down the path when a friend came up to her and asked, "Mary, how in the world did you manage to get a ride in a carriage?"

"I saw the men who stole the lace at Outwood Station, so they sent me home in the carriage after I identified them," said Mary. Her friend wanted to ask more, but by then, Nicholas was coming up the path to find her.

"What did they want with you?" Nicholas asked, looking into Mary's face.

"I saw the men who stole the lace at Outwood station," said Mary. "Why didn't you tell me?" Nicholas asked

"Well, at the time I didn't know they were the ones who had done it. I'm sorry I'm late getting home. Have the kids eaten yet?"

"I took care of them. Don't worry." Nicholas walked into the house with Mary. "Well, tell me all about it!" Nicholas pulled out a chair for Mary to sit down.

"I was at Outwood Station that morning, seeing my friend Amelia off on the train. She was going to visit her cousin in London. Well, while I was telling her good-bye, I noticed three men who were acting strange, you know, looking around a lot and whispering to one another. So when I heard about the robbery, I thought I should mention it to the inspector when he came around to work today. He asked me what I had seen while I was at the station. Mr. Alexander had told the inspector that he had seen me there that morning. I overheard one of the men say something about Henderson and told the inspector that," said Mary. "I didn't think about it much for the rest of the day until Inspector Mason arrived back at the mill, wanting me to go to Mr. Henderson's mill to see if I could point out the men I had seen. They caught two of the men at the mill, but one is still on the loose, as far as I know, so they wanted me protected until he is caught. That's why I was brought home in a carriage."

"Well, they don't need to worry about that because I don't plan on losing another daughter, so I'll make sure you are all right." Nicholas went to the sink to make a cup of tea for the both of them. "The children are already in bed, so I'll say good night."

Mary finished her last sip of tea and then headed up the stairs as well. She was exhausted and tired, and still thinking about what had happened that day. She had been scared by the look she had gotten from the one man at Henderson's mill. She certainly hoped they had caught him. If not, she was in for a restless night, worrying about it.

CHAPTER 9

The following day, Nicholas and Mary were heading for the mill when Mary noticed that Harland was going into Mr. Thornton's office. She couldn't help but smile knowing he was so close to her. Nicholas frowned when he saw the expression on her face but didn't say anything. Mary went to the weaving looms, and when the break was called, she noticed that Harland was still there. She told Nicholas she would see him later, and that she was going to visit Margaret at the house. Nicholas frowned again because he had wanted to talk to her about what he had noticed that morning. Instead, he just nodded. Mary started walking to the house when Harland stepped out of an archway of the factory and pulled her into it. "I need to talk to you," Harland said as Mary stood on tiptoes trying to kiss him. He pushed her away and held her at arm's length.

"I can't have you expecting too much from this relationship. I want to let you know that I enjoyed the time I have had with you, but it's not going to go any further than it has. You were just a great time for me. I wasn't serious about you. I just wanted to see how easy you would be to get into bed," said Harland, laughing down at her. Mary crumbled as he held her, her eyes filling with tears.

"How could you do this to me?" asked Mary.

"It was all too easy, my dear. You are pretty, and I had a need, a need that needed to be taken care of. I am a man, after all." Harland pushed her back out of the arch and walked toward his carriage. Mary watched as he left, tears rolling down her cheeks. He glanced over at her and then climbed into the carriage. Then he was gone.

Mary walked to where the other workers were having their break but was too upset to finish eating anything or to even talk to anyone as she inwardly sobbed. Nicholas frowned as he approached her. Mary knew she could never tell her father what had happened between Harland and her because her father would do something that would cost them all. No, she would keep it to herself forever. When Nicholas got to her, Mary said that she was feeling a little tired. He seemed to accept that. Nicholas still wondered about Henderson and Mary, and he was going to watch Mary closely from now on. He would see where she went, just in case there was something between the two of them. Nicholas never trusted a master totally, even if he did respect Mr. Thornton.

Several months later, at Wilfred Wilson's mill, Stevens stood by the cotton waste, puffing on his pipe. He was on a break and everyone else had gone outside on their break, so no one would notice if he smoked a little. *How could it hurt anyone?* Stevens thought to himself. The cotton fibers were blowing around through the air, flying around inside the mill. The day had already been so long, and there was a full load of work still to be done after the break was over. As Stevens took another puff of his pipe, he thought of his two children at home. They were sick, and he had been staying up to help his wife take care of them at night. He was so tired and had been spending his nights wiping sweaty foreheads and feeding the children broth for the past several weeks. They had fluff in their lungs from working in the mills from such a young age and breathing in the cotton fibers that blew around in mill. Stevens leaned against the piles of cotton and was contemplating his children's lives as he took another puff of his pipe. Smoking had become one of his few pleasures in life of late. His eyes started to droop as he relaxed against the soft cotton. Before long, he had fallen asleep. His pipe fell from his hand and landed in the cotton waste. The cotton caught fire and began to burn slowly at first, but then it became more abundant. Stevens slowly slumped to the floor of the mill as the smoke started to become thicker. Unaware of what was happening around him, he slept through the first part of the fire starting. Feeling he was getting rest at last, Stephens happily slept on the floor of the sorting room.

Meanwhile, Margaret was walking across Marlborough Mill's yard when she smelled the faint scent of burning wood and stone. She looked to the sky and saw smoke coming from the direction of Wilson's mill. She ran into the house, and Mrs. Thornton was standing there. She was on her way to the mill to alert John.

"There's smoke over by Wilson's mill!" said Margaret. Mrs. Thornton nodded and said, "We have to go tell John."

John was coming out of his office and into the factory, was heading for Nicholas's spinning mule, when he heard Margaret running into the factory. Close behind her was Mrs. Thornton.

"John, you need to come at once!" said Mrs. Thornton. Margaret had a concerned look on her face as she waited for John to speak.

"What's wrong? Has something happened to Fanny?" John asked, alarmed.

"No. There's smoke coming from the direction of Wilson's mill!" said Margaret. "They might be needing help!"

Nicholas came over when he heard what they were talking about. "Master, how can I help?"

"I want you to help Finn run things while I am gone. Hopefully, nothing tragic is going on over there." John headed for the door. Margaret, Mrs. Thornton, and John left as Nicholas went to find Finn to tell him what was going on.

Mrs. Thornton went back to the house to watch over Fanny. Fanny had needed her more lately to help with things as her pregnancy progressed. Fanny would come and spend the days at their house so she could be watched over until Watson was home at night. Fanny's being at their house was easier on Mrs. Thornton than traveling back and forth each day because of her duties at the mill.

John summoned the carriage to be brought around, and Margaret went into the house to get some blankets. John caught Nicholas coming back with Finn and asked him to inform Henderson, Slickson, and Hamper what was happening. Finn proceeded to the mill while Nicholas left to inform the other masters. John sent Nicholas in his second carriage, as that would be faster than his walking. Margaret came out of the house with her arms full of blankets. John helped her into the carriage, and they headed for the mill. They noticed the smoke had gotten worse as they glanced out the windows.

"Oh, John, it's on fire, I just know it is!" said Margaret, starting to worry. John looked at the smoke again and sighed. He too knew it was on fire. There was going to be extensive damage when they arrived. John wasn't going to say that to Margaret, though. He could tell she was already worried enough, and he knew that she knew some of the workers.

Nicholas was arriving at Mr. Henderson's mill when he noticed that Mr. Hampers was there as well. He saw that they were talking together. He got out of the carriage and went over to them. Horatio snarled, "What are you doing here?"

Nicholas stated, "Mr. Thornton has sent me to tell you he thinks there's a fire at Mr. Wilson's mill, and he wants you to go help him," ignoring Horatio's attitude. Harland looked up to the sky and saw the bellowing smoke coming from Wilson's way.

"Oh my God! Horatio, look at that!" Harland pointed to the sky. "Come on. We have to go right now!" Harland grabbed Horatio by the arm and pulled him to the carriage.

Nicholas got back into his carriage and headed for Mr. Slickson's mill while Harland and Horatio got into their carriage and headed for Wilfred's mill. "That smoke is really bellowing. I wonder if there will even be anything left to burn by the time we arrive," said Horatio, looking out the carriage window as it rambled down the street. Two water wagons went rushing by, ringing their bells as they wove between carriages on the thoroughfare.

"No doubt there is going to be extensive losses," said Harland as the mill came into view.

Margaret and John arrived just in time to see workers rushing out of the mill. As Margaret stepped out of the carriage, John ran into the mill, where he saw all the cotton bales burning in the storage area. Tiny pieces of cotton were flying through the air. Some of them lit on fire, giving the image of little fireballs in the air. Two children were huddling in a corner under a spinning mule, trying not to breathe too deeply but were starting to cough. John could scarcely make out their shapes in the smoky room. Margaret, not thinking, had followed John into the mill. She was rounding a burning jenny when she heard a scuffle. Turning sideways, she saw Stevens crouching by some cotton bales.

"What are you doing in here? Why haven't you left?" asked Margaret, squinting to focus on him. "Are you wanting to get burnt up?"

Stevens looked at her through sorrowful eyes "Missus, I didn't mean to do it," he said.

"What have you done?" Margaret asked, hardly able to breathe in the smoke as she coughed some. She walked closer to him and bent to help him up. "Come on. We need to get out of here." She pulled on his arm and led him out.

"I caused the fire! I dropped my pipe into the cotton waste by accident!" said Stevens, his face smudged from the ashes blowing in the air. Margaret stopped pulling on his arm as she turned to look at him, color draining from her face.

"What possessed you to do that? Hadn't John warned you about smoking in the sorting rooms at our mill? So why would you ever do it again?" Margaret jerked his arm.

"I just wasn't thinking right, I suppose," said Stevens, stumbling in the smoky room. Margaret was going to comment again as she saw John guiding out some children. He came around a row of spinning mules and saw Margaret standing there with Stevens. He turned to the children and said, "You kids run out that way to the front and get out of here." He pointed in the direction they should run.

John turned back to Margaret and said, "Why are you in here? You could have gotten hurt!" John grabbed her hand because he noticed their exit was closing in fast with the fire burning all around them. "Come on. We have to get out of here!"

Pieces of the ceiling started falling around them as they ran as fast as they could to the front of the mill. Stevens followed them out and up the hillside to safety. Margaret looked at the burning mill and then at Stevens with tears streaming down her face. John grabbed her and turned her to face him. "What would I have done without you?" As John quickly pulled her into his arms, Margaret looked over his shoulder at Stevens. Noticing Margaret's silence, John released her and noticed she was looking at Stevens. "What is going on here?" He looked from one to the other. "Stevens, we have to make sure everyone got out of the mill." John grabbed Stevens by the arm and led him back down the hillside.

Just before the roof collapsed, they checked to see that no one was left inside the mill. Margaret followed them with her eyes. Suddenly, she heard crying and turned her attention to the hillside. There were about three hundred people. Most of them were scratched up and bleeding, and some even had bad burns on their faces, legs, and arms. Farther down the hillside were the bodies of the dead. She noticed some children wandering around like they were lost. *The poor little ones*, she thought as she went to help Dr. Donaldson with a child who had been burned on the arm. Dr. Donaldson had been making his way through the people checking everyone out.

Margaret finished wrapping the child's arm and then went with Dr. Donaldson to help the others.

Before long, the fire had overtaken the mill. There was little need to have it put out. Margaret saw John and Stevens coming back up the hillside. Stevens's wife arrived and ran to him and started crying on his shoulder. Margaret bristled as she stared at Stevens with his wife. He had caused all of this. It was entirely his fault, and some people had died because of him. Yet here he stood with his wife, only blackened on the face by the ashes. Stevens caught her cold stare as he was holding his wife. John came over to her and noticed the way she was looking at Stevens.

"What has he done to you?" John demanded to know. Margaret slowly broke her glance and turned to John. Tears started coursing down her face again.

"Stevens caused the fire," said Margaret. "He was smoking in the sorting rooms." John's face clouded with anger and he charged down the hill at Stevens. He grabbed Stevens by the shirt as his wife screamed, "Stop it! Please, stop it! He's not doing anything!"

John looked at her and said, "He started the fire." Mrs. Stevens's mouth dropped open. John drew back his fist and started punching Stevens in the face, knocking him down on the hill. Some workers started rushing at John. Margaret started running down the hill to John's side, shouting, "He's just upset! He's just upset!" The workers started punching John to get him off of

Stevens.

"Stevens set the mill on fire!" shouted Margaret at them. Some of the men looked at Margaret and then grabbed John and shoved him out of the way. The men then started beating Stevens with their fists. Some of the inspectors started charging up the hill to stop the fighting. Margaret went to John to look at his face, which had some cuts.

Margaret took out her handkerchief and wiped away the blood. "You were right to have beat him up," said Margaret. Looking at all the workers who would now be out of work, she said, "He has ruined a great many lives today with his carelessness!" Margaret took John's arm, and they made their way down the hill. They were close to the bodies of the dead when Margaret caught a face among them that she recognized. "Oh, John! It's Elizabeth Smith! She lived near Nicholas!" Margaret was going to say more when she realized that lying next to her were the three children as well. "The children are dead as well!" Margaret started to cry and knelt beside them to cover their faces.

John's heart went out to the husband who was sure to find out soon that he had lost four members of his family. John felt in his heart the sadness of the people around him. He bent down to help Margaret up and put his arm around her and started guiding her down the hill. Mr. Smith was coming up the hill as they started down. He had still been out sick, so he wasn't there when the fire broke out. He glanced at Margaret as they passed each other. John led Margaret to the carriage. It had been the quickest way to get to the fire when they had seen the smoke bellowing across the skyline through the window at home. Mr. Wilfred Wilson was standing there looking at what remained of his mill, which was practically a shell now.

John went over to Wilson and said, "Come see me tomorrow. We'll figure out what needs to be done to rebuild it." He put his hand on Wilfred's shoulder. Wilfred turned to look at John but said nothing. He just stared as if he were numb and dazed. Wilfred turned back to his mill burning down to the ground, the ashes falling like raindrops, filling the sky with dark, dusty flakes. Margaret climbed into the carriage and waited for John. She noticed his face was bleeding again as he climbed in.

"Your poor face. You were so brave going into the mill to rescue the workers, and then on the hill, fighting Stevens the way you did." Margaret put her handkerchief on the blood again. She admired John's courage, which had come to his aid more than once before, Margaret suspected. Margaret's touch on his cut made him catch her hand and look lovingly into her eyes.

"You put yourself at risk today going into the mill like that," said John, looking slightly irritated.

"I suppose I did. But I was worried for your safety. I couldn't stand by and let you go in alone." Margaret touched the side of his face.

"It would break my heart to lose you," said John, cuddling her hand.

"I'm not going anywhere," said Margaret, smiling at him. "Now, lean back. I will hold this on your cut until we arrive at the house." John leaned back, content to have her touch on his skin. Then realizing he was exhausted, he closed his eyes and rested for the remainder of the trip. Margaret could see the fire still smoldering in the skyline, causing shadows on all the surfaces below, displaying an eerie view.

Mrs. Thornton had been waiting for them to arrive back at the house, nervous to find out what had happened over at Wilson's mill. She had been watching over Fanny all day, who was now on bed rest and couldn't be left alone for long periods of time. "John will know what to do when they arrive at Wilson's mill," Mrs. Thornton kept telling herself as she paced the floor. She thought she heard the gates opening and rushed to look out the window. The carriage entered the yard, and she watched as John stepped out and then Margaret. Mrs. Thornton decided to go down to meet them. As she opened the front door, John and Margaret were coming up the steps. Seeing John's face, Mrs. Thornton rushed to assist him.

"I'm fine mother," said John as he waved her off and continued up the steps. Margaret, coming in behind him, had her handkerchief in her hand. It was covered in blood.

"It's quite a cut," said Margaret to Mrs. Thornton. "I thought you would know what to do. He's just being stubborn about it. Dr. Donaldson was at the mill, but John wanted him to help the workers, so it is up to us to fix his face." Mrs. Thornton then sent Jane to get some bandages and cloth to clean the cut.

"Sit down here," said Mrs. Thornton, taking charge. "What were you thinking, not listening to Dr. Donaldson or Margaret?" Jane entered with the cloth and bandages. "Put them down here." Mrs. Thornton pointed to a small table by the chair. Jane placed them on the table and left to get tea for everyone. Margaret assisted Mrs. Thornton as she cleaned and then bandaged the cut. Jane arrived with the tea just as Mrs. Thornton was finishing the bandages. "You may take them back now," she said to Jane, handing her the cloth and bandages. Margaret proceeded to pour the tea for everyone when a bell rang. Fanny needed something. "Margaret, will you go see what she wants while I talk to John?" asked Mrs. Thornton.

"Of course." Margaret left the room.

Looking at John, Mrs. Thornton asked, "What caused the fire?" "Stevens and his pipe," said John.

"That fool. Why am I not surprised? It was in the back of my mind the whole time you were gone. Knowing that Wilson had hired him after you got rid of him, I expected that he was the cause of it," said Mrs. Thornton, disgusted. "What's to be done about it?"

"Wilson will have to rebuild, at a great cost, I am sure. I meet with him tomorrow to discuss all the arrangements," said John.

"Well, you look exhausted. You should go to bed." Mrs. Thornton helped him to his feet. "We'll talk tomorrow." They both left the room. Mrs. Thornton went to see how Fanny was getting along as John went off to his room.

Margaret was sitting in a chair near Fanny, starting to nod off, as Mrs.

Thornton entered. "She has fallen asleep again," whispered Margaret. "Thanks for checking on her. John told me the cause of the fire," said

Mrs. Thornton. Margaret just looked at her, exhausted herself. "Why don't you go on to bed? John has already gone up."

"I think I will." Margaret got up and walked to the door. "I'll see you tomorrow then." She made her way down the hallway to John's and her room.

John was sitting on the side of the bed, half asleep. Margaret came over to the bed and took off his shoes. She pulled the covers down on the bed and leaned him back onto the bed. Grabbing the side of his shirt, she unbuttoned it, pulled it off, and put it in the pile of clothes to be washed the next day. Some of the blood from his cut had gotten on the shirt and soaked through to his skin. Margaret grabbed a cloth by the bowl of water, wet it, and carefully washed the blood off his chest. But trying to pull off his britches proved to be a bit more difficult, as he had fallen totally asleep now. Margaret gently pulled them off and added them to the pile. She bent over him to wash the ashes from his legs, ankles, and arms and slowly covered him up. Margaret went to the bowl and cleaned herself, threw her clothes on the pile, and put on a nightdress. She climbed into bed and blew out the candle. But her mind wouldn't rest as she thought about the fire, the people on the hillside, and the faces of the Smiths and of Stevens. John was sleeping soundly, his soft sounds echoing in the bed next to her. She turned to look at his face. She could tell in the moonlight that his face seemed slightly swollen where the cut was bandaged, but other than that, he looked very much like the authoritative man she had come to love so very much. Moonlight danced across his face as she studied his features. She would never get tired of looking at him. *Having him next to me is the greatest treasure I could ever possess*, thought Margaret as she slid closer to him. Hearing his slow, calm breathing and the closeness of lying next to him had her drifting off to sleep in no time, but thoughts of the blazing fire and the outstretched bodies of the lost lives still swirled in her mind. She had fitful, horrific dreams. She tossed and turned in her sleep throughout the night, causing her to hit John's cut, waking him.

CHAPTER 10

One month later, John was crossing the yard on his way to his office when a man approached him. "Master, I wonder if I could talk to you," the man, Jacobson, asked. John looked at him for a moment and then said, "Follow me to my office." John walked into his office and sat down behind his desk. Jacobson stood in the doorway of the office, wringing his cap in his hands as he waited for Mr. Thornton to look up at him and say something. John was moving papers around on his desk, looking for some receipts for a bulk of cotton that had been ordered. Finally, he looked up and asked, "What is it that you want?

"I need a job, sir," said Jacobson. "I'm a steady man, and I will work very hard for you. My wife is a good weaver; she needs a job as well. We just moved here from another manufacturer town. We have heard about how the mills around here are cleaner than most."

"Why did you leave the place you were?" Thornton asked.

"My wife was having a hard time with the jennies there. They kept breaking down, and she was always blamed. But it wasn't her fault, Master. That the machinery wasn't sound." Jacobson looked at his feet. "I heard you were a fair master and thought I would try here."

"If that be the case, I would be glad to take you and your wife on. But you must make sure to keep to your hours, or I will have no recourse but to relieve you of your spots," said Thornton.

"Thank you, Master." Jacobson bowed and left the office, walking through the mill's sewing rooms where workers were busily working and out the doors that led to the outside courtyard.

Meanwhile, Margaret stood looking out the window at the workers below, watching as they did their various jobs. She had come to the realization that the people below struggled every day to make ends meet, and here she was, standing in this grand house, watching them struggle. She knew that some people thought themselves above all this and didn't even stop to consider what the less fortunate around them were going through. This thought had engulfed her mind lately when she thought of some of the masters she had met in the last several months when she had gone with John to sort out problems in the other mills. John to a certain degree had always considered his workers in some of his endeavors, but some of the other masters treated their workers just like the slaves in the South. At least that is how it appeared to some of the reporters who traveled to Europe. They had come to see how the mills in Europe were run and then made reports about them in America. They talked to the masters here in Milton and the other manufacturer towns.

Margaret was deep in thought when Mrs. Thornton entered the room. She had been visiting Fanny and had just returned. "Well, how do the workers get on?" asked Mrs. Thornton as she sent Sarah to get her some tea.

"They appear to be carrying on." Margaret turned to look at Mrs. Thornton as she joined her at the window. Margaret and Mrs. Thornton were so similar, though neither one would ever admit that. They both had strength of character that compelled them to act with their heart at all times. "How is Fanny getting along?" Margaret asked.

"She is doing well. I wish she had more strength about her, though. She is going to need it when the baby comes."

"Well, I'm sure she will find it when she truly needs it," said Margaret, trying to be cheerful. But the truth was, she wondered about that as well. Fanny seemed so delicate at times, reminding Margaret of her mother's disposition.

"Watson was arriving at the house when I was leaving, so Fanny wasn't too upset to see me leave. I think she was in great spirits," said Mrs. Thornton.

"Well, I hope she keeps her high spirits. It will help her as she gets closer to the end of her pregnancy, I should think," said Margaret. "I see John coming; it must be close to dinner by now." She looked at the clock on the mantel. John then entered to tell them both that he was going to be in a meeting that evening with Watson, and that Watson and Fanny were coming for dinner.

"I just left Fanny a little while ago, and she didn't say anything," said Mrs. Thornton, irritated.

"I don't think Fanny knew about it. I had just discussed it with Watson earlier today when I saw him in town," said John.

"I'll need to let the cook know," said Mrs. Thornton." This is certainly short notice, John." She gave him a stern look and then went to talk to the cook. She knew the cook wouldn't be too happy about it with such short notice. Making plans well ahead of the meal was necessary for things to run more smoothly.

Just one hour before, as Mrs. Thornton was leaving Fanny's house, Watson had arrived home. He saw Fanny sitting in the drawing room and walked toward her, hanging his hat on a hook by the door. He smiled at her. "You are looking better than you did this morning when I left." He leaned down and kissed her cheek.

"I do feel better," said Fanny.

"We are going to John's tonight. I have a new enterprise to discuss with him, so he invited us to dinner. I thought you might enjoy visiting with the ladies while I talk to John."

"Yes. I want to find out if Margaret received those new songs from her cousin, anyway," said Fanny. "By the way, what is this new enterprise you were speaking of?"

"I have gotten an offer to invest in a cotton plantation in America from that guy Sanderson we met in York. You remember him, don't you?" Fanny nodded.

"It could turn out to be quite profitable for us," said Watson.

"Oh, that sounds good," said Fanny as she became distracted in choosing a cover to wear. The truth was, if it had anything to do with cotton, Fanny found it a rather boring subject. Watson watched her as she got her cover, realizing she would never care about the things he did. But at least she seemed to love him, and that was enough for him. *And she keeps a good house*, he thought as he glanced around the room. Watson loved Fanny very deeply now and couldn't imagine not having her by his side. And he was getting excited about the baby as well. Fanny finally looked up at him and said, "I'm ready now. Let's get going before the thoroughfares get crowded with carriages for the evening." Rising up on her tiptoes, she kissed him on the cheek. Watson held the door open on the carriage as Fanny climbed up the steps and settled into the carriage seat. Watson climbed in after her, and they were off to Marlborough Mills.

They arrived at the door just as the servants were putting the food on the table. Mrs. Thornton was standing beside the table as Fanny walked into the room, carrying a dessert of custard. Nellie, one of the servants, took it from her to place on the sideboard. Fanny looked a little tired but seemed in good spirits. Watson pulled out her chair so she could sit down and then took a place next to her. "So how is business going?" asked Fanny, looking at John as Nellie placed a biscuit on her plate. She continued staring at him as she waited for his response.

"We have been having some problems, but nothing that can't be handled." John glanced at Margaret. "You have never been interested in business matters, Fanny. Why the sudden interest?"

"Well, I'm starting to find cotton more interesting." Fanny smiled at Watson, who was slightly shocked by her interest. He thought that maybe she was starting to care about business now and that maybe his earlier thoughts had been incorrect. John, noticing the exchange of glances between Fanny and Watson, frowned and then asked Fanny, "How are you doing today? Do you feel all right? You look a little tired to me."

Mortified that he thought she looked drained, Fanny replied, "I just get tired every once in a while. I have had a restful day, and I'm working on the baby's room a little bit at a time so as not to tire myself. But I feel fine." Looking at Margaret, she said, "I'm wanting to do the room in Middle Eastern colors. You know, oranges, reds, and browns."

"I'll help you if you want," said Margaret, suddenly concerned that Fanny might overdo it.

"That would be great and also would give me some time to rest as I need," said Fanny. Watson and John finished eating. Noticing the ladies were busy talking about the baby, they excused themselves and went into John's study to talk.

"So what was it you wanted to talk to me about?" John asked, as he went around the billiard table to get the sticks and set up the balls.

"I have an investment," said Watson.

"An investment? Are you serious? You know how I feel about risking my money on schemes."

Watson raised his hand at John, motioning for him to be quiet.

"Just listen to what I have to propose and then you can decide. I have a friend from America who came to England a little while ago to do various transactions. His name is Sanderson. He owns a cotton plantation and is looking for investors in the cotton fields he owns. It would defray some of his costs in getting the cotton processed. We could stand to make a hefty profit from the cotton when it comes to Europe to be sold to the cotton mills. He has had problems with some of his workers and thought that investing could help him get more workers as well. Come on. What do you say? It could be a very sound investment."

John leaned against the window, looking at Watson for a moment. Finally, he said, "I'm concerned. I have heard talk of a war between the States, and if that were to happen, what would happen to the investment?"

"Oh, Sanderson says that it is only talk, and that he doesn't think it will come to war. He says it's just a bit of bickering, is all. It is just political sides of an issue that it concerns, nothing major. He doesn't think that anything will happen that would interrupt cotton production," said Watson.

"Well, I still have my doubts. If war were to break out, and depending on where it breaks out, the cotton fields might be destroyed. It could also cause exports to be delayed," said John. "I'm sorry, but I'm not going to risk my payroll right now. Give it a couple of months to see if war breaks out in America. Then we can decide if it would be wise to invest."

"Well, I don't know how long Sanderson will wait, but I will contact him and find out." Watson frowned at John and left the billiard room to go to Fanny. He was disappointed that once again John had refused him. Upon seeing his face, Fanny knew that John had refused him. "Fanny, are you ready to go?" asked Watson.

"Yes. Margaret is going to come and start helping me tomorrow." Fanny picked up her cover and told Mrs. Thornton and Margaret goodbye.

"Fanny, take care of yourself," said John to her back as she and Watson left.

"What was all that about?" asked Mrs. Thornton. "Watson's up to another investment scheme," said John. "You didn't want to join this one?" asked Mrs. Thornton.

"No, I'm afraid this one won't turn out the way Watson wants it to." John then turned to Margaret and said, "He is going to invest in American cotton."

"Oh my. What is he thinking? Aren't there rumors of war?" asked Margaret. But before John could answer, Mrs. Thornton said, "John, you could be right on this one." Frowning, she thought about what could happen to Fanny if the investment didn't turn out well.

Several months later, war broke out in America. Many of the cotton plantations as well as cotton mills were burned down by opposing sides of the war, causing great loss and devastation to the countryside. Sanderson's plantation was taken over by the Union soldiers, and he was wounded in the leg by gunfire and taken hostage by the North. The president of the United States, Abraham Lincoln, put a blockade on all Southern exports of cotton to Europe so he could try to help with the costs of the war for the North. He thought he could help the Union troops by trying to sell the cotton to areas not affected by the war, funding the North's causes with weapons and supplies. In the end, European cotton mill owners had to rely on Egyptian and India cotton for a while, whose costs were too high for some of the mills. During those very hard times, harder than they had been before the Civil War, only one-eighth of the mills were able to work full-time, and there was such a shortage of cotton coming to the mills, they had to cut down on hours of operation, causing even more distress to already distressed workers, who were barely making it before the Civil War began. The unemployed workers, however, supported the North in the war because the working conditions of the slaves weren't that different from their own.

Watson regretted the investment as the months went by, as he started losing large amounts of money from the investment he had so believed in. Even after the Civil War, the cotton supplies from America were still very uncertain, and he had suffered great losses from cotton mill fires and raids on the cotton plantations in America.

CHAPTER 11

As the months passed, workers started complaining about their wages and working conditions. John left the mill to go have a meeting with the masters. He needed to see what progress had been achieved in making the mills more productive for the workers. He entered the meeting hall to find Horatio and the others already there. Wilfred's mill was finally running again after much work and labor from the workers to rebuild it. Stevens and his family had been run out of the town, and the workers were back at their own mills, working again.

"Silas, I understand you didn't listen to what we discussed at the last meeting, so you were fined and now your workers have it in for you. That was a stupid move on your part, don't you think? You will be lucky if they don't strike on you next," said John.

"They'll learn their place yet," said Silas.

"Be careful that you are not the next person run out of town, Silas," said John, irritated.

"You are really trying to risk it all, aren't you"? said Harland, frowning. "Do you really think it could come to all that?" asked Silas, looking at the

other masters.

"It very well could," said Horatio, shaking his head.

"Well, I think you have gotten the message from us all. Be on your guard, and try to work it out with your workers, Silas, before it's too late," stated John. "If you get fined again, it could mean jail time for you."

"Harland, I have heard rumors of you and Mary Higgins, a worker from my mill. Is there any truth to them?" asked John

"No. She is nice, but I don't want any entanglements," said Harland, grinning at the other masters.

"Harland, it would be looked on in a very unkind light. Don't start something that could cause the masters social disgrace, do you understand? Drop her, now! Do you hear me? As magistrate, I can tell you, you could actually be jailed for such behavior," said John. Harland lost his smile.

"Don't worry. I have already told her that I'm not interested," he said. "Now, Horatio, how is it going setting up a meal place for your workers?"

John asked. "The children need full stomachs to have fit minds to do their work and their studies. That's the only way we masters are going to make a profit in the long run. It will encourage the workers to stay with us longer and work with us for more years. Even if their wages are low, they will be thankful for a food kitchen to eat in. And it's a manageable endeavor for us masters to invest in."

"I have started building it in the back of the children's study building. It should be up and functioning in about a month, I should think," said Hamper.

"That's very good," said John. "Well, is there anything else we need to discuss at this time?" The other masters shook their heads. "Well, all right. We will meet again in a couple months then." John headed for the door.

He was just arriving home as Margaret was headed out. "I will be back later. I'm going to Fanny's now." Margaret kissed his cheek and hurried down the stairs to the carriage below and climbed inside.

Fanny was in the dining room eating a late breakfast when Margaret arrived. Seeing Fanny alone, Margaret asked, "Where is Watson that he would leave you alone to eat?" Fanny's eyes lit up when she saw Margaret had arrived.

"Will you join me? Watson had to go to a meeting with some people. I don't know who," stated Fanny.

"Well, I have already eaten, but I will join you in some tea, of course," said Margaret. "Maybe I'll have a roll as well. How are you feeling today?" Margaret started to nibble on the roll.

"I'm actually a little tired. I didn't get much sleep last night. The baby wouldn't stop moving, so I couldn't get comfortable all night. But fixing up the baby's room will get me energized again. I just love what I have gotten done with the room so far."

"How do you get the energy? It has been so hot and humid, and you have been on bed rest for months now," said Margaret.

"Oh, I find that if I rest for several hours, I can then do things in preparation of the baby for several hours before I need to rest again." Pausing a little, she continued. "I'm being careful, Margaret. Really I am."

"I know you'll be glad for the baby to be born, won't you?" asked Margaret.

"Oh, yes. You've guessed right. He is quite the kicker! It's a wonder I'm not bruised on the inside!" said Fanny, laughing.

"How do you know it's a boy?"

"Because I think a daughter wouldn't be so hard on me," said Fanny, smiling again.

After breakfast, they headed to the baby's room. As they walked through the house, Margaret noticed it had Indian papers from the exhibition a year and a half ago, and they gleamed as if they were still new, which was a real achievement for Milton, considering how much smoke was always in the air that seemed to dull most papers and fabrics in a house. When they reached the room, Margaret noticed it was already wall washed but still needed papers on some of the walls and pictures put up, as well as furniture brought in and the bed set up. The only piece of furniture in the room was a rocker, which Fanny sat down in immediately. "The papers shouldn't take too long to put up. I only want them on the top part of the wall, near the ceiling." Margaret walked over to the papers and found the paste to attach them to the wall. She slowly rolled out a piece of the paper and started putting the paste on it. The paste was made from a mixture of water, starch, and some other things that seemed to get sticky quite fast. Margaret brushed it onto the paper and started putting it on the wall. She was halfway through when Mrs. Thornton arrived, bringing some fruit for Fanny. Fanny and Margaret had tittle-tattles during the afternoon, and when Mrs. Thornton arrived, it was time for a break.

"Margaret, why do you look so tired?" asked Mrs. Thornton, frowning. "You look a bit drained! Maybe it's time you took a break."

Fanny looked closer at Margaret and then frowned as well. "Margaret, you do look a bit tired. I hadn't noticed before." They all sat down to have tea and started talking about the progress of the baby's room.

"I think you made a good choice with those papers," said Mrs. Thornton. "Yes, when I saw them at the exhibition, I just couldn't resist. I had a

feeling I would need them," said Fanny, smiling at her mother.

"Well, they certainly look good in this room," said Margaret, smiling. "You know what? I really do feel a little tired! Do you mind, if I go lay down for a while?" Margaret began to look pale. Mrs. Thornton frowned and stood up to take her to one of the extra bedrooms. Fanny always kept some ready for any company that may come to visit unexpectedly or after a long journey or trip. They walked up the stairs and down the hall to a room that was decorated with floral patterns in burgundy and pink with cream lace borders. The room wasn't very big, but it looked very comfortable for one guest. There was a bowl on a table for water so one could wash up and a pitcher beside it. Mrs. Thornton helped her to the bed, as Margaret was starting to feel a little faint.

"Here, lay down, and I will get a cool cloth for your forehead," Mrs. Thornton said. She walked to the table and poured some water into the bowl. After wetting a cloth that was lying next to the bowl, she brought it to Margaret. "This will probably help you. How long have you been feeling like this?"

"I've been feeling this way for several days. It's not serious, I'm just a little tired, that's all. I must have worked too hard at the food building yesterday." Margaret took the cloth and leaned back, placing it on her forehead. "I'll just rest for about ten minutes. I'll be right back downstairs to help with the room some more."

"All right," said Mrs. Thornton, still a little concerned. "I'll leave you then and check on Fanny. Get some rest!" She then shut the door and went back downstairs. Fanny was sitting on a cushioned chair in the sitting room when Mrs. Thornton entered.

"How is she? Is she all right? Did I tire her out with all my requests for the room?"

"No. I think it's something else. She is looking too pale for just being tired. I'm going to send Dr. Donaldson a message, saying he should come over here to check on her," said Mrs. Thornton.

"Should we notify John? I can send a servant to let him know what is going on," said Fanny.

"No, there's no need to bother John right now. He's in another meeting anyway. We'll notify him if it turns out to be serious. Let's just wait and see what Dr. Donaldson has to say." Mrs. Thornton sent a servant to contact Dr. Donaldson. Soon the servant returned to say that Dr. Donaldson would come to the house shortly. He had some other house calls to make on the other side of town, so he would come later.

Meanwhile, Mrs. Thornton went to the baby's room to finish the papers and get the furniture moved in. Fanny supervised the placing of the different pieces of furniture about the room. They were just finishing up when Margaret came down the stairs.

"How do you feel?" Mrs. Thornton asked, noticing her first. "Oh, I feel a lot better," said Margaret, yawning a little.

Fanny smiled as she searched Margaret's face for any paleness. "You do look better," said Fanny, smiling.

"Yes, you do," said Mrs. Thornton.

"I told you. I was just a little tired from the work," said Margaret, looking at them both like they were crazy to have been so worried about her. "I only needed rest to refresh me."

CHAPTER 12

One week earlier, Dr. Donaldson had just opened his office when Mrs. Helena Roberts arrived with her daughter, Miranda. "Helena, what are you doing here today?" asked Dr. Donaldson.

"It is Miranda, Doctor. She has been coughing all morning," said Mrs.

Roberts.

"Well, bring her into this room, and I will get my instruments." Dr. Donaldson pointed to a room on his left. Going back into his office, he retrieved his instruments and then shut his office door. Dr. Donaldson found Miranda sitting on the table sucking her thumb with Mrs. Roberts standing close by. "Let's give a listen to you," said Dr. Donaldson, putting an instrument to her chest and then moving it around her chest slowly, listening closely. Her breathing sounded like crinkling paper, and when she coughed, it rumbled on the left side of her chest. Looking at Mrs. Roberts, Dr. Donaldson told her, "She doesn't sound good. Did she by chance get caught in the downpour of rain we had yesterday?"

"Yes, she did. She and her brothers had been outside playing when it had started to rain. I was exhausted from work and had fallen asleep in a chair when they came in and woke me up. I'm not sure how long they were out in the rain. I was sleeping so soundly that I didn't even hear the rain until they woke me up, dripping wet. I took off their clothes right away, warmed them by the fire, and had them put on dry clothes. The boys appear to be fine, but Miranda here has been coughing since then." Mrs. Roberts looked beaten down. Dr. Donaldson patted her shoulder and told her that Miranda probably had caught pneumonia and would need bed rest and medication.

"I want you to give her this four times a day," said Dr. Donaldson, handing her a brown bottle. "And if she gets hot, give her this as well." He handed her a blue bottle. "Give her only a teaspoon of each, all right? And don't give her the fever medicine more than every eight hours. Give it only if she gets hot." Mrs. Roberts nodded and then picked up Miranda and headed for the door. Dr. Donaldson told Mrs. Brown, his secretary, "Put this visit on her bill, Mrs. Brown." As they were leaving, a young man arrived at the door of the office. Taking his hat off as Mrs. Roberts and Miranda exited, he bowed as he held the door for them. Stepping inside, he extended his hand to Dr. Donaldson, introducing himself as Dr. James Murray.

"It's nice to finally meet you, Dr. Murray," said Dr. Donaldson. "I wasn't expecting you to arrive for another week. I thought you hadn't finished your finals yet. According to the professor at the university, they couldn't let you come until next week. But I'm really glad you are here now. It's gotten very busy around here." Dr. Donaldson smiled at him.

"Well, I was a top student at the university, so the professor allowed me to take my tests early. I hope I'll have time to freshen up a little before I have to start, though," said Dr. Murray.

"Oh, don't worry about that. You don't need to do much today. You'll really be starting tomorrow. Let me show you to your place. It is located on the top floor of this building. It makes it easier to get to work on time. I find that to be true, anyway. I live on the floor below you."

"Well, that certainly works out great, doesn't it" said Dr. Murray, picking up his bags and walking up the steps. They climbed several flights of stairs when they arrived at a door located at the end of the stairway. "This looks like an odd way to end the stairs," said Dr. Murray, looking at the door with a small landing patio.

"Yes, this is a small tenant house that takes up the entire top floor," said Dr. Donaldson, opening the door with a key and then turning to hand the key to Dr. Murray. Dr. Donaldson led him into a sitting area, where there were several pieces of furniture and a tall clock in the corner. Walking through the place, Dr. Murray saw that there were six rooms in all: a sitting room, a bedchamber, an eating area, a kitchen, a private bathing room, and a study. Looking at Dr. Donaldson, he expressed his pleasure at such a nice accommodation.

"I knew you would like it. If there are things that you need, don't hesitate to let me know. There are several young ladies who would be willing to run and get anything you may need for the house. All you have to do is let me know, and I will send one of them on the errand," said Dr. Donaldson, smiling. He then left to go back downstairs to his office and to the other patients he had waiting for him.

Dr. Murray said to Dr. Donaldson's back, "I will be down later after I have settled in just to check out the office. All right?"

Dr. Donaldson looked back up at him and said, "All right. I'll see you later. Get settled in now. We'll talk later." He waved and continued down the stairs.

Turning back into the house, Dr. Murray decided to start in the bedchamber first, taking all the covers off the furniture and bed and wiping down the areas where the dust had collected. Then he put away his clothes in the side shelves, placed his empty bags at the bottom of the shelves, and closed the door. Climbing onto the bed, he rubbed his eyes and soon fell asleep on the pillows he had brought with him. Several hours later, he woke to the sound of scraping in the sitting room. Getting out of bed, he walked into the sitting room. After some investigating, he found that the pendulum of the tall clock in the corner had caught in a side chain, causing it to scrape against the clock casing. After fixing it, he decided that since he was awake, he would change his clothes, wash his face, and go down to the office. Grabbing his key and putting it in a pocket of his vest, he shut the front door and made his way downstairs. Dr. Donaldson was just coming out of a room as Dr. Murray walked down the hallway.

"Did you get some rest, or did you work on your rooms?" asked Dr.

Donaldson.

"I did a little of both actually," said Dr. Murray, smiling.

"Well, if you're ready to start work today, I could use you help now. I have a patient for you to look at." Entering the closest room, Dr. Murray found a young man with a nail sticking through his hand, blood spreading through a dirty piece of cloth he had wrapped around the wound. The young man was holding the cloth in place with his other hand.

"What happened to you?" asked Dr. Murray, walking over to the young man.

"I was loading the wooden crates of cotton onto a train at the station when one of them came apart in my hands, and a nail got stuck in my hand," said the young man.

"Let's take a look and see how it looks when I remove the nail, although you leaving the nail in place probably caused you to lose less blood. You would have lost more blood if you had pulled it out right away. That was very wise of you." Dr. Murray slowly unwrapped the cloth and looked closely at the puncture wound. He handed the young man a stick to bite down on and then called for a nurse to assist him. He then pulled out a tool of his bag and slowly pulled the nail out of the young man's hand. The young man squirmed in pain but didn't yell out. "Young man, what is your name?"

"The name's Sam, sir."

"Well, Sam, I believe there wasn't too much damage done to your hand. I have given you two stitches, and you will probably have some swelling. I'm going to give you something for the pain, and the nurse will clean it and bandage it up for you. Rub this ointment on it twice a day." Dr. Murray handed him a red jar. "I recommend that you not try using that hand for several days."

"But, sir, I can't afford not to be working," said Sam, frowning.

"Well, I'm afraid you aren't going to be able to work for several days.

Perhaps one of your coworkers will cover for you while you are gone?"

"I'll see if I can get my friend George to cover for me, and then I won't lose my spot," said Sam.

"That's the spirit," said Dr. Murray, patting him on the back.

"Excuse me, sir, but I couldn't help noticing your accent. Where are you from?" asked Sam.

"Scotland," said Dr. Murray, smiling.

"Well, I wouldn't have thought you would come to a place like this then," said Sam. "We are all English here, you know." He quickly pulled away his good hand when Dr. Murray tried to shake it. Sam went out the door and turned back to look at Dr. Murray with disdain. "Dr. Donaldson, I can't believe you would let a Scottish person take care of your patients! What were you thinking?"

Dr. Donaldson looked at Sam for a moment and then asked, "Did he treat you badly?"

"Well, no. He did a good job with my hand. But he's Scottish, Doc!" said Sam.

"If he treated you well, should it matter where he is from? I needed help, and he was willing to come, no questions asked, to help me here in Milton. Besides, his family knows all about the hardships of cotton, and I know he understands the struggles in this town. If you are unhappy with your care, come tell me. Otherwise, don't complain to me about a brilliant doctor who was the top of his class and will be of great help to me." Dr. Donaldson showed Sam to the door, frowning.

Meanwhile, Dr. Murray stood in the room, speechless at what had just happened. It hadn't occurred to him that the English people in this town might not welcome a doctor who was from Scotland. He wouldn't volunteer that information anymore unless asked, of course, but he wasn't about to hide who or what he was either. He was a Scotsman and proud of it. He overheard Dr. Donaldson defending and felt a little bit better knowing that Dr. Donaldson was on his side.

The day went rather smoothly after that. Dr. Donaldson and Dr. Murray made house calls as well. It was troubling to Dr. Murray at how many of their patients were having lung problems because of the cotton mills. The sick children were the hardest for him to take care of because he knew many of them would never be adults. One of the calls took them to Nicholas's home. Knocking on the door, Dr. Donaldson turned to Dr. Murray and told him a little about the family and the Boucher children as they waited for the door to be answered. They knocked again, and Jenny came to the door. Standing in a pale flowered dress, she said to someone over her shoulder inside the house, "The doctor is here."

"Come in, Dr. Donaldson," said Mary as she set the table for dinner. "Hello, Mary. I would like to introduce you to Dr. James Murray. He has

come with me tonight. I hope you don't mind. I am showing him around. He is my new assistant doctor," said Dr. Donaldson.

"I understand you have a little one who is still sick," said

Dr. Murray, smiling at her, noticing her shiny long hair as she came around the table to shake his hand.

"She is upstairs in the big bedroom, Dr. Donaldson," said Mary as she took the stairs, leading them to the bedroom. Entering the room, they found Emma lying on a small lower bed, sweating and coughing loudly. Dr. Donaldson went over to her, opened his bag, and pulled out his stethoscope. Dr. Murray looked around the room, which was really small, considering they called it the big bedroom. There were faded and worn papers on the wall, which probably had been nice when they were new. There were four small beds, two above the other two. There was a small table with a little shelf under it with two candles. But except for those items, the room was completely bare. There appeared to be several broken toys in one corner, but that was all.

Looking back at Dr. Donaldson, Dr. Murray noticed that Emma was struggling to breathe. Dr. Donaldson looked up at Dr. Murray and said, "I don't think she will last much longer. Her lungs are too congested. You better go downstairs and ask Mary to come back up, and Nicholas as well, if he has arrived home." Nodding, Dr. Murray did as instructed. Dr. Donaldson said something soothing to Emma and held her hand as he waited for the others.

Going downstairs, Dr. Murray saw the other children playing on the floor. Then he turned to Mary and a man sitting at the table, who he assumed was Nicholas, and told them that they needed to come upstairs. Nicholas and Mary went up to the room, telling the children to remain playing where they were. They entered the room to hear stuttering breaths coming from the bed. Nicholas touched Dr. Donaldson's shoulder and then sat on the end of the bed to talk to Emma

"Honey, it's all right. I'm right here. And Mary's here too." Nicholas touched her cheek and held her hand. Memories of his daughter, Betsy's death started floating through Nicholas's mind. Dr. Donaldson got up, giving Mary room to sit down beside her. Looking up at Dr. Donaldson with tears in his eyes, Nicholas asked, "How long does she have?"

"It won't be long. Maybe a couple of hours, if that long," said Dr. Donaldson sadly.

"Emma, you are a lucky girl. You'll get to see your mum and dad soon," said Mary, trying not to show too much emotion. Looking at Nicholas, she said, "I need to let her brothers and sisters know. I won't be long." Before she left, she brought Lizzie, Simon, Frank, Karl, and Marc from their families and sent Jenny and Thomas up to her room. Arriving a short time later with the other five children, they all stood beside Emma as she took her last breaths.

"I don't understand this," said Thomas. "She has only been sick about a week."

"She has never been sick like this before," said Jenny. "It was just too much for her tiny body."

Lizzie, Simon, Frank, Karl, and Marc just looked from Emma's little body to their feet, not knowing what to say. Mary told them to follow her downstairs. She brought them all to the table, sat them down, and gave them all some dinner. Dr. Donaldson and Dr. Murray left shortly afterward, with Dr. Donaldson promising to come back later to make sure everything was handled for Emma's funeral. Dr. Donaldson then sent Dr. Murray back to the office and his home, and then continued over to Marlborough Mills to let Margaret and John know.

The following day, everyone gathered at the hilltop to say good-bye to Emma. All of the Boucher children were there with the families they lived with. Margaret, John, and Hannah were there too. Dr. Donaldson had come to the service, leaving Dr. Murray in charge of the office while he was away.

"That's one more little child the cotton mills have taken," said Margaret, looking at John. "Can't you make sure the air is better for the workers by insisting that all the masters use the same circulating system you use at our mill?"

"I'll see what can be done," said John, pulling Margaret into his arms and kissing her forehead. Everyone started leaving the hillside. As Hannah started back to Fanny's, Margaret went over to Nicholas and Mary.

"I hope someday this will never happen," said Margaret, hugging them both and placing flowers on the grave.

"Mrs. Margaret, you were very helpful preparing for this.

Thanks for everything you did last night to help Mary. We are indebted to you, as always," said Nicholas.

"Oh, don't say that. You owe me nothing but friendship. That's what I value most," said Margaret.

"Well, you will always be our friend." Nicholas hugged her again. Then they all walked down the hill and to Nicholas's home. Giving their regards to the family, Margaret, John, and Dr. Donaldson left for home.

Dr. Murray had been quite busy that morning. He had seen twelve patients. At lunch, he went upstairs to his home. As he turned the key in the door and went into the kitchen, he saw that Mrs. Brown had sent some girls to get food for him. Opening a brown package, Dr. Murray found some ham and goat cheese. Another package held some plates and cups and still another held sugar, salt, and flour. There were several bottles of milk and a small package of tea. They had stocked most of the shelves with fruit, vegetables, and bread. On the table he found a drinking glass filled with flowers that one of the girls had given him. Sitting down at the table, he ate some of the ham and bread, drank some milk with his tea, and read a copy of the local paper, which had been left on his counter. The news in Milton was about the same type of news he read about in Scotland. Soon, he finished and headed back down to the office. Upon seeing Dr. Donaldson enter, Dr. Murray asked, "Did everything go well?"

"Yes, it was a very nice service. I went to their home afterward to pay my respects and then headed back here. Has everything run smoothly in my absence?"

"Yes. Only a few scary moments," said Dr. Murray, smiling.

"Well, if you are all right with this, since you covered everyone this morning, I thought I would cover this afternoon's patients," said Dr. Donaldson. "By the way, word has gotten around that I have an assistant, so there were several questions about that, but nothing to really speak of."

"Well, I have more things that I want to accomplish in my home, so by your leave, I would like to get a chance to do them now." Dr. Murray turned to leave and went upstairs.

CHAPTER 13

Returning once more to his house, Dr. Murray put the keys down on the table and went into the sitting room. The girls Mrs. Brown had sent up had dusted some of the furniture so that didn't leave too many things to still do in this room. Going into the bath area, Dr. Murray noticed that someone had placed some lavender-scented soap on the side of the tub. Sitting on the cabinet was a ceramic bowl and pitcher with a masculine design, making the room look perfect. Contented with the room, he went into the study. Dr. Murray saw that his books were still in the boxes, so he wiped off some of the shelves and stacked the books on the closest shelves. He pulled out an anatomy book and several medicine books and laid them on his desk so they would be close at hand for easy reference. Finished, he sat down at the desk to view his handiwork. All the room really needed now was some artwork on the wall. Amazingly, the papers in this room were appropriate to the atmosphere and what one would want in here. Stretching his arms behind his neck, he placed his feet on the desk and yawned. He was still tired from his journey to Milton. Before he realized it, he had nodded off in the comfortable chair.

Several hours later, he awoke with a start. Realizing he had fallen asleep, he went to the basin bowl to wash his face. Patting himself dry with a towel, he went into the bedchamber and looked for anything he still needed to do there. He stacked what clothes he hadn't gotten to yet. They were still lying inside his trunk. When he placed them on a shelf in the closet, he noticed a small gap in the back corner. He put his hand on the gap and felt a breeze. This was usually the area where you would sit empty trunks and bags. He walked farther into the closet to check it out. Standing in front of the gap, he put some pressure on the panel, and it started to slide to the side. It opened to reveal a small dusty room behind the closet wall. Dr. Murray realized that this was the extra space he had wondered about. When he viewed the top floor from the outside of the building, he had wondered about the missing space. It had always appeared to be larger on the outside of the building than it appeared on the inside. He decided not to mention this extra addition to his house because it could be his secret getaway spot from overzealous patients and others. Smiling to himself, he decided he would get some furnishings for it. With such a small place, no one would notice him doing it. The only problem to this plan was that he would have to have some help fixing it up. There was a small window that looked out on the backside of the town, giving a great view of some grassy meadows and trees spotted with the occasional farmhouse. Dr. Murray closed the panel of the secret room and decided to go out to see the town and its surroundings. He had not gotten a chance to see it since he had arrived. After changing into some clean clothes, he grabbed his cover and left.

Stepping out into the evening light, he spotted a boy playing with a bird that appeared to have a broken wing. The boy was trying to help it as Dr. Murray crossed the street to go into a drapery shop. The clanging of Mrs. Brown's bell notified her that she had a customer. "Hello! You must be the new doctor because I haven't seen you around here before," said Mrs. Brown, smiling at him.

"Yes, I'm Dr. Donaldson's new assistant. It is very nice to meet you. I'm Dr. James Murray." He shook her hand.

"How can I help you today, Doctor?" asked Mrs. Brown, folding up a piece of fabric from her previous customer.

"I was hoping you might have some fabric for a new pair of pants. Do you know who could make them for me?"

"I can help you with both of those things. I not only sell fabric, I am also a seamstress and can make you anything you want. I can make repairs on your clothes to make you new ones," said Mrs. Brown, smiling.

"That sounds good. I would like to have a pair of pants made out of that gray fabric right over there." He pointed to some fabric on a low shelf.

"Oh, that will do just fine for you!" Mrs. Brown picked up the fabric and measured it out for the pants. "Let me take some measurements, and then we can get them started."

"Thank you. Mrs. Brown, is it?" "Yes. Yes, it is." She smiled.

"I noticed the name on the shop and just figured you must be Mrs. Brown, seeing that you came to wait on me."

"Well, since you work for Dr. Donaldson, you must have met my sister by now." Mrs. Brown looked up at him as she folded the cloth.

"Oh, his secretary? She is your sister?"

"Yes, she and I married cousins. Her husband works at the paper, and my husband works with me here."

"That's nice, isn't it, to be so close to family? Well, when can I get my pants from you?"

"They should be ready Tuesday next," said Mrs. Brown, waving good- bye. Dr. Murray left, leaving the bell ringing behind him.

He headed back to his house and then to dinner at Dr. Donaldson's home. Dr. Donaldson had just arrived on his floor when Dr. Murray came down the hallway toward him, carrying some of the fruit for the custard dessert they would have that night with the dinner.

A week later, Dr. Murray and Dr. Donaldson were working with some patients when a message was delivered, asking them to come to Fanny's home at once. It concerned something about Margaret Thornton's paleness.

Soon after, a knock came at the door of Fanny's house. Mrs. Thornton left to answer the door, when Fanny, who was standing behind Margaret, suddenly grabbed a chair and groaned.

"Oh my! Are you having pains?" asked Margaret, rushing over to Fanny. All Fanny could do was nod as she groaned once again. Margaret helped her sit down and then rushed after Mrs. Thornton to tell her what was happening.

"Oh, thank God! Dr. Donaldson, you are right on time!" said Margaret, not realizing he was there to see her and not Fanny.

"This is Dr. James Murray, my new assistant. He is the one you asked about at Emma's funeral. He has moved here to Milton to do his residence by helping me with my patients." Dr. Donaldson motioned toward to the young doctor who had entered the room behind him. Margaret nodded to him, said, "Nice to meet you," and then turned to Dr. Donaldson. "Fanny is in the sitting room. Her pains just started!" She pointed to Fanny as they entered the room. Mrs. Thornton caught her breath as she realized what was happening and closed the door behind the doctors. They all went to the sitting room, and Dr. Donaldson started checking Fanny's vitals.

"She has started her pains all right, but it is still too soon for her to have the baby. I don't think the baby will survive unless we can keep the little one in there for a little bit longer," Dr. Donaldson said, looking at Dr. Murray.

"What do we need to do?" asked Mrs. Thornton

"We need to get her in bed. Hopefully, that will stop the pains," said Dr.

Donaldson.

Margaret and Mrs. Thornton helped Fanny up. She groaned as she tried to walk up the stairs. "I can't. I'm in too much pain," she cried.

"Is there a room down here we can take her to?" asked Dr. Donaldson. "Watson has a bed in his study," groaned Fanny. They turned and headed

down the side hallway. Dr. Murray picked Fanny up and carried her to the room as Margaret opened the door.

"Here you go," said Margaret. Dr. Murray placed Fanny on the bed. "Emily, come in here and light some candles and open the curtains so

some light can come in!" shouted Mrs. Thornton as she smoothed and folded down the bed.

Watson arrived at the house with John right behind him and realized no one was in the sitting room. "Where is everyone?" called Watson from the doorway.

"We're in here," called Margaret. "Fanny is having pains."

Watson and John entered the room just as Dr. Donaldson was giving Fanny something to drink. "Fanny, you will need to lay flat on your back and not sit up for at least a day. Hopefully, the medicine you just took will help stop the pains so you won't have the baby yet," said Dr. Donaldson. "If this works, she will need to stay in bed for the rest of her pregnancy. If she gets up at all, she may start having pains again. We want her to keep the baby in there for at least two more months where it will then have a chance of living. If she makes it to the end of her complete pregnancy, I will be very surprised."

"I would be really surprised if she does make it that long, but let's hope she can make it for two months at least," said Dr. Murray, picking up the syringe they had used to medicate her and then closing Dr. Donaldson's bag.

"Fanny, I will stay the night just to be on the safe side, if I can get a room to rest in," said Dr. Donaldson. Looking over at Dr. Murray, he said, "James, you can go back to the office alone and see any afternoon patients for me." Mrs. Thornton called for Ellie and told her to make up a room for the doctor. Everyone except Watson left the room and headed for the sitting room.

"Margaret, now what is going on with you? I had actually come here because of you. Hannah had a message brought to me," said Dr. Donaldson. "What is this all about?" asked John, alarmed. Coming up to Margaret, he

put his hand on her waist.

"I was just feeling a little tired today, that was all," said Margaret, smiling up at him. Seeing his alarm, she said, "Really. I am just fine."

Dr. Donaldson instructed her to sit down, and then he started checking her. "Hannah said that you were looking quite pale. Is that true?"

"Maybe a little. But wouldn't I look pale if I'm just tired?" asked Margaret.

"No, not usually. But you appear to be fine now. However, I'll just see if you start feeling that way again." Mrs. Thornton looked from Margaret to John and said she would be spending the night so they could go back to the mill without her. John went to get their covers because it had been raining earlier. Mrs. Thornton and Dr. Donaldson left the sitting room to go back to Fanny.

Dr. Murray looked down at Margaret. "So do you like living here in Milton?"

"Yes, I have grown quite attached to the town," said Margaret, smiling. She stood up as John came back into the room. When he looked at her, he noticed that she was pale.

"Are you all right? You look pale?" Now he noticed her shaking a little. "I'm just starting to feel a little dizzy, that's all. Probably the excitement

from Fanny's condition." Margaret grabbed the top of a chair as Dr. Murray came over and had her sit back down.

"She looks like she did earlier today," said Mrs. Thornton, walking back into the room. "That's why I sent for Dr. Donaldson to start with."

"I am just fine," said Margaret. She started to put on her cover and head for the front door.

"Well, all right," said John, following her out.

"I'll just head to the office then," said Dr. Murray as Dr. Donaldson entered the hallway. Margaret was almost to the carriage when she fainted and fell to the ground. John in horror ran to her side, followed by Dr. Murray. John picked her up and carried her back into the house. Dr. Murray followed him into the house and told him to lay her on the sofa. Mrs. Thornton, hearing all the commotion, came back into the sitting room with Dr. Donaldson.

"She fainted by the carriage. What is going on with her, Dr. Donaldson?" John asked, looking quite worried. Both Dr. Donaldson and Dr. Murray went over to Margaret. Dr. Donaldson listened to her heart while Dr. Murray checked her other vitals. John moved back to give them room.

"Why did she pass out?" asked John. Just then, Margaret started to stir.

She opened her eyes to see everyone staring at her. "Why are you all staring at me like that?"

"You fainted by the carriage," said John. "You scared me. I thought you were dead!" A tear welled up in his eye.

"Margaret, have you eaten today?" asked Dr. Donaldson.

"Yes. In fact, I am always feeling hungry the last couple of days," said Margaret.

Dr. Donaldson looked at her and smiled. "Well, it seems to me that maybe this is an illness that will be cured in about nine months," he said.

"What are you telling us?" asked John

"I'm saying she's perfectly fine. She's just pregnant." Dr. Donaldson smiled at them as Margaret's mouth dropped open and looked up at John.

"Oh my!" said John. He pulled her up into his arms, kissing and squeezing her tight.

"I guess that means you are happy about it?" said Margaret

from within his arms. She smiled when she noticed the tears in Mrs. Thornton's eyes. John finally let her go and turned and shook Dr. Donaldson's hand as well as Dr. Murray's. Then he turned to Margaret, saying they needed to leave, for he had to let people know he was going to be a father. Margaret laughed when she saw how happy he was. Watson, hearing the laughter, poked his head out of his study to ask what was happening and then went back inside to tell Fanny. Margaret went to tell Fanny good-bye before they left.

"Oh, Margaret, this is excellent news! Our babies will be able to play together!" said Fanny, smiling weakly as she fought against another pain.

"I will come see you tomorrow," said Margaret. John was already at the front door waiting for her as she came back down the hallway. Taking her cover from him, she followed him out to the carriage and climbed in, laying her head on his shoulder to rest while they traveled back to the house.

Sarah came down to the carriage as they arrived at the mill yard.

"Can I carry anything inside for you?" she asked.

"Mrs. Thornton is staying with Fanny tonight because she started having pains, so everything was left at Fanny's house. I will bring the extra things home tomorrow," said Margaret as she handed her covers to Sarah to put away. Margaret went into the sitting room and asked Sarah to bring in some tea. John told her he had to check on the mill and would be back a little later. Sarah came into the room with tea and some scones.

"Sit it right there, Sarah," said Margaret, pointing to a table.

"Will there be anything else, Mrs. Margaret? If not, I will go have my supper now," said Sarah.

"Yes, go have your supper." Sarah started to leave the room. "By the way, Sarah. I'm going to have a baby." Margaret smiled as she said it to someone for the first time. Sarah told Margaret she was very pleased for her and then left. Margaret decided to go lay down in her room for a while and picked up her tea and carried it to her room. As she climbed onto the bed, she had hardly laid down when she fell fast asleep. She rested peacefully, content with the knowledge that her baby was starting to grow inside her. Every tiny part created a design of the love she felt for John in its every feature and showing the strength it was certain to have as John's child.

The following day, Margaret arose to the sound of the mill already at work. Sarah was just looking in on her when she woke.

"Mrs. Margaret, can I get anything for you? You seemed so tired that Mr.

Thornton said to let you rest." "What time is it, Sarah?"

"It's a little after eleven, Missus."

"Can you get me something to eat? I'll be down in just a bit," said Margaret. "And oh, Sarah. Where is Mr. Thornton?"

"He's at the mill, Mrs. Margaret." Smiling, Sarah then left the room. Margaret got out of bed and went to the bowl on the table to wash her face. She decided to wear her blue dress and bonnet and then went downstairs to the dining room. Nellie was just setting some scones and jellies on the table. Sausage and butter already sat on the sideboard. Margaret sat down just as John entered for some tea.

"I see you are up! How are you feeling this morning, my dear?" John asked, smiling down at her.

"I feel well," said Margaret. He sat down across the table from her and started pouring himself some tea. Margaret busied herself buttering a scone while John watched her movements. Margaret caught him watching her and smiled. "What are you thinking about? I can tell you have something on your mind."

"I was thinking that now that I am finally used to you being mine, you are giving me another great gift, that of a child. I feel like a very, very lucky man," said John, almost breathless with emotion. His eyes showed how very much he cared for her. Margaret cherished that look in his eyes. It was the only time she felt she could almost see into his soul.

"You know, I don't need so much praise from you. I haven't always treated you with the kindness you are showing me right now." Margaret blushed and looked down at her food.

"I know that to most people I appear to be a hard man, but with you, I just somehow melt inside. You totally intoxicate me, Margaret." John stood and came around the table, pulled her out of her chair and kissed her. Then he let her go and abruptly backed away. Clearing his throat, he said, "I had better get back to the mill before I lose the money you invested by not returning to work at all today." Smiling mischievously, he turned and left the room. Margaret watched him leave, blushing and putting her fingers to her lips, smiling at the thought of him. Nellie returned to the room to clear the table, and Margaret went to get her cover. She walked across the yard to the street and then through the cemetery on the hillside. She saw Elizabeth's grave as she passed the cemetery and went down the hill to Nicholas's home.

Margaret knocked on the door and waited for it to be answered. The door opened to show Jenny Boucher standing there. "Hello, Mrs. Margaret! Nicholas and Mary are not home yet. Will you come in and wait?" Jenny held the door for her to step inside.

"Thank you, Jenny. I will wait awhile. So why are you home?"

"I'm helping in the food building today, so I'm going to head there a little later."

It was almost one o'clock when Nicholas finally arrived at the house. When he entered the room, he saw Margaret and said, "I hear that congratulations are in order!" He hugged her and put his hat on the table.

"Did John already tell you?" said Margaret, looking a little disappointed. "Yes, he's been talking about it all day to the workers," said Nicholas,

laughing. "I think it's great. I almost feel like I am getting a grandchild."

Looking from Nicholas to Jenny, Margaret said, "Well, I need to be going. I had a lovely visit with Jenny, and I want to check in on Mary at the food building. I was just waiting for you so I could tell you about the baby." Margaret smiled as she headed for the door.

"I'll see you again soon then." said Nicholas, opening the door for her. Margaret started walking back up the hill to the cemetery when she saw

Andrew Smith standing by the stones of his wife and three children. Going up to him, she asked, "How are you doing, Mr. Smith?"

Looking around, he said, "I'm dealing with it the best that I can. It's always there in my head, reminding me of their voices." He grabbed her hand. "I want to thank you for being a friend to my Elizabeth and for everything that you and Mr. Thornton did during the fire. A lot of people were saved because of you two." Turning back to the stones of his wife and children, he knelt and put his hand on Elizabeth's stone. Margaret silently walked away, thinking about what a sad circumstance the fire had been. She continued on down the hill to Marlborough Mills, the gates open and beckoning her. When Margaret entered the yard, Mary came running up and threw her arms around her, congratulating her on the baby.

"Thank you, Mary," said Margaret, smiling. "I'm very happy and so is John. Apparently, he's been telling all of our friends. I'll talk to you later, for now I need to get a carriage to go see Fanny. She was having pains last night."

"Bye then," said Mary, smiling. She then headed to the thorough fare for home.

Margaret summoned the carriage and was climbing in just as John came out of the mill. "Where are you going?" John called after her. Margaret stopped on the step of the carriage and said, "I'm leaving to see Fanny and if your mother is coming back here tonight."

John walked up to the carriage and said, "I'll come with you. I need to speak with Watson, and I want to see Fanny as well." Margaret stepped into the carriage with John right behind her and they headed for Fanny's home. Looking out the window, Margaret noticed Mr. Smith walking home from the cemetery.

John looked over at her at that same moment and noticed her watching the man out the window. "Do you know him?"

"Yes, that's Elizabeth Smith's husband. You know, the woman who lived near Nicholas? Elizabeth and their three children died in the Wilson fire. He was at the graves earlier today. I spoke briefly with him. He's so sad, and I just feel so sorry for him." Margaret watched him disappear into the street below.

"I feel for him too. It would be terrible to lose your wife and children." John pulled Margaret closer to him on the seat. Margaret looked at John and smiled. He was becoming her whole life. He was the strongest man she had ever met, stronger than her father had ever been. Fanny was sleeping soundly when they arrived. Mrs. Thornton said that her pains had stopped during the night and that she was doing better. Watson came into the room and smiled.

"She's going to be fine. We just need to keep her in bed, without her complaining too much. Dr. Donaldson thinks she'll make it through her pregnancy," said Watson.

"Well, we came to see her. Can I go in?" asked Margaret.

"Yes, you can look in, but don't stay long. She needs her rest," said Mrs. Thornton. John walked over to Watson, and they started discussing the investment. Margaret looked in and saw Fanny was still asleep. Not wanting to disturb her, she went back into the sitting room. Mrs. Thornton was telling John that she would be staying there for a while, so they didn't need to worry about her. Margaret touched Mrs. Thornton on the shoulder.

"She was sleeping so soundly. I didn't want to disturb her." Mrs. Thornton smiled. "How are you feeling today?" Smiling back, Margaret said, "I'm doing well, thanks."

John looked at his mother and said, "Since Fanny is sleeping, I guess we'll head back to the house. I'm finished speaking with Watson, so we can go." Mrs. Thornton for the first time reached over and hugged Margaret good-bye. Margaret, surprised, just smiled. Mrs. Thornton was not one to show affection very often; maybe Margaret was starting to wear off on her. John looked surprised as well.

"Good-bye. I will send a message if we need anything or if Fanny starts having pains again," said Mrs. Thornton. She waved to them and left to get some tea to take to Fanny's room.

"You are starting to look tired again," said John, looking at Margaret next to him in the carriage.

"Well, it's been a long day," said Margaret, slightly smiling, as she rested her head on his shoulder. She closed her eyes on the trip to Marlborough Mill, and swaying with the carriage's movements, she fell asleep.

Within a week, Mrs. Thornton had returned to the house, as Fanny's bed rest seemed to be working. Margaret, not needing to stay close to the house, started taking her walks again. Visiting Nicholas and Mary during afternoon breaks from the mill had become sort of a ritual with her. She looked forward to the time she spent with them and not have to concentrate on the mill or finances or life and its hardship for others (except visiting Nicholas was always a reminder of life's hardships). She would sometimes visit Nicholas' daughter, Betsy's grave and leave flowers. Helping Mrs. Thornton with a few things around the house had given Margaret a better understanding of her, especially on the days when it was raining and it wasn't good to travel. John kept busy with the mill and some nights stayed in his office going over shipments and other details, having meetings with the other masters, and attending to his magistrate duties.

Several months passed. Mrs. Thornton and Margaret were once again going to visit Fanny. She was sitting up in bed reading the latest fashion news from London when they arrived. Looking up from her news, Fanny smiled and said, "Dr. Donaldson was here yesterday and said I can start going into the sitting room for tea each day if I want to."

"Oh, that is good news!" said Margaret, coupled with Mrs. Thornton. "Well, it's almost teatime now. Do you want me to help you to the sitting

room?" asked Mrs. Thornton.

Fanny smiled at her mother. "That would be lovely." Margaret went around to one side of the bed while Mrs. Thornton went to the other. They helped Fanny up and then guided her to the sitting room. Mrs. Thornton called for Ellie to bring in the tea and then took a seat opposite Fanny. Margaret sat down next to Fanny, and they both started looking at the new fashions in the paper. Ellie entered with the tea, sitting it on the table next to the sofa. Margaret reached for the teapot and started pouring them all tea. Mrs. Thornton poured milk into the cups and then handed one to Fanny and one to Margaret. Then picking up her own cup, she started sipping it. Fanny was talking of the fashions in London and saying, "After the baby is born, I'll be able to wear some of these." She pointed to a couple of dresses in the paper.

Mrs. Thornton looked across the table at the paper and said, "You'll look fine in those, Fanny." Fanny looked up at her mother and smiled. Margaret was admiring them as well. Finishing their tea, they got Fanny up to take her back to her room.

Suddenly, Fanny stiffened and caught her breath. "Oh my. I've started having pains again." Looking at her mother, she said, "Send for Dr. Donaldson. This is it." Mrs. Thornton called for Ellie and told her to take a message to Dr. Donaldson to come quickly.

Margaret helped Fanny to her room and got her on the bed. "Lay down.

I'll see if your mother has sent for the doctor yet."

Mrs. Thornton met her halfway down the hallway. "I have sent for the doctor."

Several minutes later, a knock came at the door. Nellie answered the door as Mrs. Thornton and Margaret went to Fanny. Nellie then led Dr. Donaldson and Dr. Murray down the hallway to the room. She let them enter the room first and then announced their arrival.

Dr. Donaldson went over to the bed and said, "All right, let's see what is going on." He checked Fanny out and said, "She's going to have this baby soon. Go get some water and cloths ready. James, you get on the other side of her. You can help me with this."

Mrs. Thornton looked at Ellie standing in the doorway and gave her orders for the water and cloths and then turned to Margaret and told her to go get Watson and John. Watson was just returning to his office when Margaret arrived in the carriage and told him what was happening. Watson immediately called for his carriage and headed for his house. Margaret left to go to Marlborough Mills. John was coming out of the mill when Margaret arrived. She leaned out of the carriage and shouted to John, "Come at once! Fanny is having the baby!"

John hurried to the carriage and climbed in as he shouted to Nicholas to watch the mill while they were gone. When they arrived at Fanny's home, Mrs. Thornton met them at the door and told them Fanny was having problems delivering the baby. They all rushed into the house and found Watson pacing the hallway.

"Watson, what has the doctor told you?" John asked.

"The baby's head appears to be caught inside of her. Both Dr. Donaldson and Dr. Murray think it may be too big for her to deliver."

About an hour later, they heard a loud scream and the weak cry of a baby. Watson rushed to the door, and Mrs. Thornton went into the room. John asked Ellie, "What is happening in there?" Ellie just shook her head and went down the hallway with some bloody cloths. Moments later, Mrs. Thornton walked out with a bundle in her arms.

"You have a son," said Mrs. Thornton, handing the baby to Watson. "Fanny is very weak. Dr. Murray is having a hard time stopping her bleeding. Dr. Donaldson delivered the baby." Putting her hand on Watson's shoulder, she said, "Pray for her. That's what you need to do now. And please keep the baby warm." She then went back into the room to see how Fanny was doing. Seeing Fanny's face, Mrs. Thornton remembered when she had given birth to her.

One minute later, Mrs. Thornton came out and asked Margaret to come into the room with her. As Margaret entered the room, Fanny motioned for her to come to the bedside.

"Margaret, promise me, if anything happens to me that you and Mother will make sure that Watson does right by our son," said Fanny.

"Don't worry. We will," said Mrs. Thornton before Margaret could answer.

"You're going to be fine," said Margaret, holding her hand and smiling, although the fear in her eyes was evident.

"Thanks for being here, Margaret," said Fanny. "It means a lot to me." Margaret squeezed her hand and then told her to get some rest. She laid

Fanny's hand back down on the bed.

Mrs. Thornton looked from Fanny to Margaret and said, "Margaret, you go on out. I will stay here with her. You're looking tired. Go sit down for a while."

Dr. Murray finished cleaning his equipment and turned to Mrs. Thornton. "I finally have her bleeding under control, but she's going to need a lot of rest." Then pausing, he asked, "Is there someone to take care of the baby for several weeks so she can regain her strength?"

"I will hire a nanny immediately," said Mrs. Thornton. "I'll make sure that the servants look after Watson as well." Turning to Fanny, Mrs. Thornton said, "I need to talk to everyone. I'll be right back, Fanny." Looking at Dr. Donaldson, she asked, "Can you stay until I make all the arrangements?"

"Yes, I'll be staying for the time being. I have to keep a close eye on her bleeding."

Mrs. Thornton walked out of the room and down the hallway to tell everyone what was being done. As she entered the sitting room, everyone stood up.

Looking at John and Margaret, she said, "I will be staying here for a while. There is nothing more to be done except wait, so you both can go back to the house when you want." Turning, she called for Ellie. When Ellie entered, Mrs. Thornton said, "I need you to tell the other servants that they need to help Watson in whatever he may need for the next several days. I need you to help with Fanny and get one of the other servants to do your other duties for you for a little while at least. Margaret, when you get back to the house, send Jane over here to help me and have Sarah help you with the house."

Dr. Donaldson came into the sitting room to tell Margaret that he would like to have her pregnancy taken care of by Dr. Murray. "I feel that Fanny is going to need my attention for now, and Dr. Murray is very capable of taking care of any of your needs. I hope that is all right with you. I trust him, and he is really good," said Dr. Donaldson, touching her hand.

"That will be fine. If you have trust in him, I certainly have no objections to it." Margaret patted his hand and got up to leave. Dr. Murray was coming into the room as Margaret was getting her cover to leave. "Dr. Murray, Dr. Donaldson tells me you are to be my doctor now. I look forward to seeing you soon then." Margaret shook his hand and bowed before leaving to go back to the mill.

When John and Margaret arrived back at the house, Margaret sent Jane in the carriage to Fanny's house. She then called in Sarah and told her, "You will be running the servants while Jane is gone, and I will help you when needed."

Meanwhile, Mrs. Thornton sent a servant to get Rebecca, a well-known nanny, to come to help with the baby. Watson stood holding his son and decided to go into the room to show him to Fanny. "Mrs. Thornton, do you mind if I spend a little time alone with Fanny?"

"That would be fine. I'll be just outside if you need anything," said Mrs. Thornton. She closed the door and left.

"Fanny, what do you want to name our son?" asked Watson,

looking at her. Smiling weakly, Fanny said, "I thought we would name him Peter, after your father."

"I love that idea. Father would have loved that. I'm just sorry he never got to meet his grandson. How are you feeling?" he asked, touching her hand as she stroked the baby's cheek.

"I'm tired and I feel really weak. Do you mind if I rest awhile? Please take Peter with you, and give him to Mother. I'm sure you still have work to do. She can watch him until Rebecca comes," said Fanny weakly.

Closing the door behind him, Watson then took the baby to Mrs. Thornton and said Fanny was resting. Looking up at Watson, Mrs. Thornton asked, "So what is his name?"

"We named him Peter, after my father."

"Well, welcome to the family, little Peter," said Mrs. Thornton, rubbing his chin with her finger. Looking down at his face she could almost see Fanny there. The eyes were the same, but the hair was like Watson's.

Rebecca arrived later that day and took Peter with her to the nursery. Having checked in on Fanny, Mrs. Thornton went to have a cup of tea in the sitting room. Watson was going over papers for his new work when she entered the room.

"I hope that work doesn't keep you from giving Fanny the attention she needs right now," said Mrs. Thornton, frowning over at his bent back as he leaned over his work, concentrating on some figures in a document.

CHAPTER 14

One month later, Watson stood in Dr. Donaldson's office holding Peter in his arms. The baby was running a fever and was coughing. Dr. Donaldson had Watson lay the baby on the examination table and started listening to him. He could tell by the congestion in Peter's lungs that he must have pneumonia and could easily die from the smoky atmosphere that surrounded Milton.

"It's not good, Watson. He's congested in his lungs, and with him being

born early he could easily die from it. Why did you bring him here? You could have sent a servant to get me," said Dr. Donaldson.

"I'm sorry. I didn't know what I needed to do, Doc. Fanny would be good at this, but not me," said Watson.

"Fanny is still fragile and weak, Watson. She doesn't have the strength to help you yet. You're going to have to take Peter out of the town, perhaps to London, where the air is cleaner. If you can't leave yourself to take him, send the nanny with him to London. I'll give you medication for him, but it won't do any good if you don't get him out of town immediately. This is your son. You need to take care of him, Watson." Dr. Donaldson handed him the medicine and led him to the door of the office and out the building. He then called after Watson, "Make sure you get him out of town as soon as possible. I'll be over later to check on Fanny."

Watson looked down at Peter's little face and pulled him to his chest. "I don't know what I am doing, Peter. This is something your mother was meant to do. I don't know how to care for you. I'm just not used to being around babies." Then patting Peter on the back, he said to himself, "Fanny will know what to do. She will know how to arrange everything." Climbing into the carriage, Watson shut the door behind them. Peter looked up at his father, who was lost in his thoughts and staring out the window. Sticking his thumb in his mouth, Peter closed his eyes and fell asleep.

Mrs. Thornton was entering the yard just as Watson arrived in his carriage. Getting out of the carriage, Watson motioned to Mrs. Thornton as she climbed out of hers. "What's going on? Why do you have Peter with you? Where is the nanny I hired?" asked Mrs. Thornton.

"I had Rebecca stay with Fanny while I took Peter to the doctor. He is running a fever and has been coughing," said Watson. "Dr. Donaldson said he has pneumonia and is having a hard time breathing. I am going to make arrangements for Rebecca to take him to London for a while. Dr. Donaldson fears he will die if we keep him here because of the constant smoke in the air."

"Why in the world did you take Peter out in the air? You should have just sent the servant for him!" scolded Mrs. Thornton, taking Peter from him.

"I wasn't thinking. I was just so worried about him and Fanny. I was not in my right mind at the time." Watson looked miserable.

Mrs. Thornton squeezed his arm and told him, "It will be all right. I'm here to help." They walked into the house and heard Fanny calling, "Watson, is that you? How is Peter?"

Mrs. Thornton walked into the room followed by Watson. "Fanny, we're here. I met Watson as he was arriving. Peter has pneumonia. We have to send him to London for a while until his health improves." Mrs. Thornton patted Fanny's hand after handing Peter to Rebecca.

Fanny started to cry. "My poor baby!" Then calling for Ellie, she turned to Mrs. Thornton. "I don't want him to go without me. Ellie, get my things ready at once. I have to leave with Peter right away. His life depends on it!" Mrs. Thornton was about to tell Fanny she couldn't go with the baby when Dr. Donaldson arrived. "Dr. Donaldson, I'm going to leave with Peter at once for London," said Fanny.

"Well, let me check you first. I need to see if that's a good idea." Dr.

Donaldson bent over her and listened to her heart.

Coming to the bedside, Mrs. Thornton said, "She is still weak. I don't think she needs to be traveling anywhere." Dr. Donaldson stood up and looked from Fanny to Mrs. Thornton.

"I'm afraid I'm going to agree with your mother. You are in no condition to be traveling. I'm sorry, but you will have to stay here for now." Dr. Donaldson patted Fanny's hand.

Tears started to well up in Fanny's eyes. Watson said, "I know you don't like Peter going to London without you, but it's got to be done for his health and you must stay here for yours." As he came to Fanny's side, he said, "Dry your tears now. You need to keep up your strength so you can get well."

"I'll make sure he gets the best of care while he is there," said Mrs. Thornton, looking over Watson's shoulder. Ellie, who had been standing there the whole time, was told to go pack Peter's things. "Rebecca, you need to pack your things as well, so please hand Peter to me and go along and pack. You will leave tomorrow morning on the train," said Mrs. Thornton, dismissing the servants. Mrs. Thornton then went to the rocking chair and started rocking Peter to sleep. She could feel his chest rumbling as she rocked him. Fanny watched from the bed as Peter sucked his thumb and fell asleep.

Reaching out to the baby, Fanny said, "Mom, hand him to me. I want to hold him since he's leaving for a while." Handing Peter to Fanny, Mrs. Thornton sat back down again. Fanny slid down in the bed and lay next to Peter and started rubbing his cheek. His cheeks were hot to the touch and flushed red as he slept next to her. *Poor little guy*, thought Fanny. She then realized she was feeling very tired as well. Putting her arms around him and pulling him close to her, she fell asleep, cuddling him. Mrs. Thornton put her finger to her lips and motioned for everyone to leave, whispering that she said she would stay and watch over them.

Watson went out to the sitting room and poured himself a scotch. Then running his fingers through his hair, he went to a chair and sat down. Dr. Donaldson sat down next to him and told him that sending Peter away for a while would be best for Peter and for Fanny, who was probably making herself weaker because she insisted on taking care of Peter herself. And because of that, she wasn't gaining her strength back. Watson looked at him and nodded, exhausted from the constant stress of worrying about Fanny's weaknesses and Peter's frailties. He felt like a heel for actually feeling relieved that Peter would be in London with Rebecca for a while, but now Watson could focus all his strength on Fanny. Dr. Donaldson stood to leave and told Watson to watch out for his own health while taking care of Fanny. He then picked up his hat and left

The next morning, Fanny kissed Peter as they got ready to leave and told Rebecca to take good care of him for her and to write her of his progress while in London. Watson bent down and kissed Fanny on the head as he left to take them to the train station. As Rebecca and Peter stepped onto the train, Watson told her that he would be coming to London in a week to check on them.

Leaving the station, Watson headed to work, knowing Mrs. Thornton and Margaret would be going to the house soon to stay with Fanny. John and Margaret had been alarmed the night before when they had found out Peter was so ill and had to be taken to London. John said he would travel with Watson to London that following week to check on them as well. He wanted Fanny not to worry about Watson on the trip. Margaret and Mrs. Thornton grabbed some baked goods to take to Fanny's and left to go visit her while John left for the mill. Fanny, feeling a little better, went to the sitting room to read her fashion news and was quite involved with it when Margaret and Mrs. Thornton arrived. Fanny looked up from her news and said, "I was wondering when you two would arrive." Smiling, she laid her news on the table next to her chair.

Surprised, Mrs. Thornton said, "You must be feeling better today, coming out here to the sitting room."

"Has Rebecca left with the baby yet?" Margaret asked, sitting down next to her.

"They left a little while ago. Watson took them to the station and then was heading to work," said Fanny. "I hope I feel better next week so I'll be able to go with John and Watson to see them." Margaret and Mrs. Thornton glanced at each other.

"So, Fanny, you must be feeling better. You don't look as pale today," said Margaret, smiling.

"I'm feeling better, although I still feel tired. How are you feeling, Margaret? Any more fainting spells?"

"I'm having moments of nausea all the time, so my appetite is down. But not too much fainting now," said Margaret, smiling again. "That was so embarrassing."

A week passed, and John and Watson went to London to check on Peter. He was doing better and would be able to return in another two weeks. Watson had hired the same doctor that Edith had used, and Edith checked in on Rebecca and Peter every day to see that everything was running smoothly. Finally, she suggested that they come to her home for the duration of their time in London so she could be there if Rebecca should need any help with Peter. Watson and John expressed their gratitude to Edith. They had returned to Milton several days later.

The town was as busy before they left as it was when they returned so no one seemed to have noticed. Rebecca returned with Peter two weeks later. Walking into the house, she and Watson found Fanny sitting in the sitting room. She was smiling and so happy to have the baby back home with her. She had stayed weak and had not been able to travel to see him while in London.

"Fanny, are you all right? You look pale to me," said Watson as he rushed to her side.

"I was all right earlier today, but now I just feel a bit tired, is all," said Fanny, reaching for the baby. Rebecca hesitated as Fanny appeared as though she were going to faint.

"I think maybe you should rest first," said Watson, watching her unsteady hands. Looking at Rebecca, he motioned with his eyes for her to follow him to the hallway. Looking at Fanny, he said, "I'll be right back. I need to see to the baby's things and give Rebecca some instructions for him." Smiling, he kissed her softly on the lips and left with Rebecca, who was still holding Peter. As soon as they were away from Fanny, he said to Rebecca, "I want you to go put the baby down for his nap and then tell Nellie to go for Dr. Donaldson. There is something wrong with the way Fanny looks. Then I want you to have Ellie go over to Marlborough Mills to get Fanny's mother and bring her here at once."

Rebecca left to do as she was told, and Watson returned to the sitting room to find Fanny slumped over in her seat. Rushing over to her, Watson yelled, "Fanny, are you all right? Wake up for me! You are passing out!" He started patting her face.

Fanny slowly opened her eyes and said, "Watson, take me to the bed. I feel so faint." Watson carried her to her room and laid her down on the bed, only to realize that she had fainted once more. Patting her on the face, Watson got her to look at him once again.

"I need you to stay awake for me, Fanny," said Watson, looking into her eyes. Slowly nodding, Fanny kept looking at him, too weak to say anything. Dr. Donaldson arrived soon afterward and came into the room. "She is too weak to speak," said Watson.

Dr. Donaldson bent down to feel her forehead. "She's burning up with fever. We need to get it down as quickly as possible or we'll lose her."

Watson shouted, "Nellie, bring lots of ice from the box, quickly!" Mrs.

Thornton arrived with Margaret behind her.

When Dr. Donaldson saw Margaret, he told her to go back to the mill. "You can't be here, Margaret. This may be contagious and you'll risk your health and the baby's. We will get a message to you when we know what is going on."

Margaret immediately left to go back to Marlborough Mills. Mrs. Thornton started putting ice around Fanny when Nellie arrived back in the room. Standing up, Dr. Donaldson looked at Watson and said, "You will need to send the baby over to Marlborough Mill. I believe Fanny has typhoid fever. See the rash on her stomach? And her fever is very high. We must check the food immediately for contamination and all the servants to rule them out as carriers of the typhoid virus."

Mrs. Thornton left to get the baby and have Rebecca take him to the mill. "Nellie, you are going to need to stay and help with Fanny. You appear to be all right," said Dr. Donaldson.

Coming back into the room, Mrs. Thornton said, "I'll stay with Fanny, Watson. You need to go tell John and Margaret that I will be staying here. Let them know that they need to keep the baby there. Take Rebecca and Peter with you. They are waiting in the hallway." Watson ran his hands through his hair and left for the mill.

Over the next several weeks, Watson came to see John and Margaret, give them an update on Fanny's condition, and check on Rebecca and Peter. Fanny was getting worse as time went by, and they were all preparing for the worst.

Finally, Mrs. Thornton sent word that Fanny was no longer able to stay awake for any amount of time. It wouldn't be long before she died. Dr. Donaldson had done everything he could. That evening, with John, Mrs. Thornton, and Watson around her bedside, Fanny took her last breath. John left the room to tell the servants. Nellie burst into tears and ran to her room. John made the arrangements as Mrs. Thornton carefully washed Fanny, combed her hair like she had when Fanny was a child and put flowers in it, and dressed her in her favorite blue dress. Watson, filled with sorrow, left to check on Peter and to tell Margaret. Mrs. Thornton once again remembered how it felt to lose someone dear to her heart and wept as she took care of Fanny.

Margaret hugged Watson as he sobbed on her shoulder with loud gulps.

Then she and John went to the church to see to the funeral arrangements.

The next day, they buried Fanny on a hillside on the outskirts of Milton near the brook that had meant so much to Margaret and John. She would be near the sound of the rippling water, singing birds, and beautiful meadows. Dr. Donaldson and Dr. Murray came to the house for a meal after the funeral, along with other friends of the family. Margaret went to a corner of the room to sit and eat. Dr. Murray came over to talk with her while John was host to the guests. "I understand you have never been to Scotland, Mrs. Thornton," said Dr. Murray.

"That is correct, I haven't. But I would love to visit there someday," said Margaret. "I understand that you are from Glasgow. You must know a little about the cotton mills then, seeing that they have mills in Edinburgh and other parts as well."

"Yes, I have cousins who work in some of the mills there. I know how hard it can be to survive while working in one," said Dr. Murray.

"Has it been hard for you to adjust to living in Milton?" Margaret took another bite of food.

"The people here were slow to warm up to me, but I believe they are coming around now." Dr. Murray smiled as he, too, ate.

"Give them time. They will see how good you are at your job. Then there won't be any problems. They were the same with me when I first came to Milton. So what do your parents do for a living?" she asked, biting into an apple.

"My dad died about a year ago from a fall from a horse. But after he died, the doctors found some lumps on his lungs. He was a musician and played the lute. My mum lives in Paisley and is a weaver for a cotton mill nearby. She works really hard, and thanks to an inheritance from my grandfather, she was able to send me to medical school in Glasgow. Then I came here to train with Dr. Donaldson."

"Do you have any brothers or sisters?" Margaret asked, looking over at John.

"I have an older brother and sister. My brother is a musician, and my sister is a teacher. I don't get to see them very often. My sister lives in Edinburgh, and my brother lives in Glasgow, not far from my mum." He nodded at John, who had just walked over to them.

"Have you two been getting acquainted?" John asked, looking from one to the other.

"Yes, we have. How is your mum doing over there? She isn't getting overwhelmed, is she?" Margaret looked over at Mrs. Thornton, concerned about how she was dealing with Fanny's death.

"I believe she has held up quite well. But maybe we should start sending people home now. What do you think, Dr. Murray?" asked John while looking for Dr. Donaldson.

"I believe that would probably be best for everyone. Margaret looks tired, and Dr. Donaldson was up all night with Fanny before she died." Dr. Murray stood and asked Sarah for his cover. He noticed Mary and Nicholas were leaving and went to talk to them.

"Margaret, help me see everyone out," said John. He guided her to their guests. After seeing everyone out, they went back into the sitting room to sit in silence for a while. Mrs. Thornton was tired and left to go to her room early. John told Margaret to go on up and he would have a drink brought to the room for her. Margaret nodded and then climbed up the stairs to their room. Sitting down on the bed, she rested her eyes a while and then laid down and fell asleep before John could make it upstairs to talk to her about everything that had happened that day and the day before.

Several months had come and gone. Finally, it felt like life was beginning to get back to normal again in the household. Fanny's death had taken its toll on everyone. It had been hard to go on with life without her there. Peter was getting stronger by the day and often brought Mrs. Thornton out of her depression, which she seemed to have been suffering since the death of her daughter. Mrs. Thornton spent a lot of time with Peter, hoping she could help him to know what his mother had been like. Although he was still a baby, she spent a lot of time rocking him and telling him stories about his mother. Watson had become a lost man, turning to drinking heavily to deal with his grief and barely could stand being around little Peter because of how much he reminded him of Fanny. John had tried reasoning with him about the dangers of getting lost in his grief. Watson had let his business run without leaving his assistant in charge and did not even know or care about how much money he had been losing in the speculation he had gotten into with Sanderson. The war had come to the States, and there had been embargoes put on the cotton exports. Watson was steadily losing everything he had put into the investment. Soon, he would be penniless if he didn't get a grip on his sorrow and start working again.

"Watson, you need to put the drink away," said John as he entered the house one afternoon. Watson had just finished off two bottles of Scotch and was just about to open another when John reached his side. Putting a hand on his shoulder, he said, "Watson, you have to start dealing with your loss. You have a son who needs you! You are all he has now."

Watson looked at John and tried to focus on his face. His eyes had become blurry and red from the sobbing that he couldn't seem to get a grip on. "I know I look pathetic, but I just can't seem to live anymore. I don't seem to exist without her here. I never realized how much she meant to me until it was too late." Watson tried to shake his head clear. He stood and clung to John. "Help me, John. I really don't like what I am becoming, but I can't stop myself."

"Look, you can start by getting the alcohol out of the house. Just try to get up in the morning. I think it's been a mistake to keep Peter at our house. I am sending Rebecca back over here with him so you can start focusing on your son and not on yourself."

"All right." Watson tripped over the chair and stumbled into it. John called to Nellie to bring some strong coffee for Watson and left him in Nellie's care. Then he went to get Rebecca and Peter.

Arriving later back at the house, Rebecca entered the sitting room to find Watson drinking coffee. "Mr. Thornton says I'm to watch out for you and Peter and make sure you can get on with your son and start doing things with him," said Rebecca.

"That would be helpful. Thanks." Watson took Peter in his arms and hugged him for the first time since Fanny had died. Rebecca poured him some more coffee and watched to make sure Watson could hold Peter without dropping him. "I will do my best with you, son. I promise I will try. You just have to be patient with me while I get the hang of this, all right?" He kissed Peter on the head.

Meanwhile at Marlborough Mills, Mrs. Thornton entered the sitting room to find Margaret standing by the window looking down on the workers. The mill had been doing quite well, and the workers seemed to be happy with the way things were run now. Margaret had been thinking about her baby and what names she liked.

"Margaret, I want to talk to you about something," said Mrs. Thornton.

Turning around, Margaret looked at her. "What is it?"

"I have noticed that you haven't had much of an appetite lately. Are you feeling all right?"

"Yes, I'm all right. It's just been some morning sickness, is all. I don't feel very well during midday hours. I always feel sick during that time of day. But it's starting to get better."

"Well, then, have you thought about what you would like to name the baby?"

"There are several names I have been thinking about, but I just can't decide yet."

"I thought you might consider the name Richard, if it's a boy," said Mrs. Thornton.

"Why Richard?"

"About six months after John was born, I got pregnant again. He doesn't know because I have never really talked about it. But I was so excited and decided right away that I would name the baby

Richard, after George's father. George had been really young when his father had died, and I had promised him I would name our next child after his father. But I lost the baby at six months. It had been a boy, and I was absolutely devastated."

"There is nothing that would make me happier then to do that for you," said Margaret, her eyes tearing up. Mrs. Thornton's face started shining, and she did the one thing most out of character for her—she walked over and hugged Margaret tightly. Then she said, "You can call me Hannah from now on."

Margaret's mouth dropped open a little and she started sobbing. "Does this mean you have finally accepted me as your daughter-in-law?"

"It most certainly does," said Hannah, smiling at her and taking Margaret's hand into her own. Margaret had never expected this moment to ever happen but was grateful for it now. Just then John walked in. He knew what had finally happened between them. Smiling, he embraced and kissed them both on the cheek and forehead.

CHAPTER 15

Business had been keeping John very busy as of late, as there had been a lot of worker versus master issues coming up. Because of the way some of the other masters were handling the problems with their workers and the wages they paid, John's magistrate duties had been taking up a lot of his valuable time, most of it unfortunately streaming from one particular master, Silas Slickson. The fool had really taken his place as a master to new heights, and was recently cited for over twelve violations concerning his workers and the conditions at his mill. Before long, all the workers would rebel or strike or worse, and John was hoping he could stop it from happening. He had been having meetings with all the masters, trying to work out some of their grievances. He had also, on Margaret's advice, decided to have several meetings with workers to hear their grievances as well. Nicholas as a committeeman had been there to try to keep the order. John was going to the inspectors office the next day to see what was being done about the citations to Slickson. Personally, John would prefer to run Slickson out of the town and replace him with a better master, but that would never happen because Slickson did quite well for himself and had a lot of following from other masters who thought his harsh ways worked best on the workers; those who, as Margaret would say, had little or no concern for the lives of their workers and viewed them as cattle to be led to the slaughter for the sole purpose of making the masters a profit. John would have to show a certain stamina and discipline in handling this situation and focus on his own confidence and strength to make the right choices and show it to the other masters as he sorted it all out. Margaret interrupted his thoughts, saying she was going to bed and asking if he would he be up soon. He smiled at her and said, "In a moment." Setting his glass down on the side table, he blew out the candles as he made his way upstairs to their room. He washed up before turning around and climbing into bed to sleep.

The next evening, Slickson stumbled into the Golden Dragon's front door where all the workers went for a pint. Already drunk from the other pubs he had been to earlier that evening, Slickson had been shown the door at several of them for being too rowdy and loud. Inside the Golden Dragon, Nicholas was sitting in the far back corner having a pint with some of the workers when Slickson stumbled into the pub. Nicholas recognized him right away and quickly looked at the man sitting next to him. Templeton had worked for Slickson for several years and knew firsthand the cruelty at the hands of a master. Most of Slickson's workers were talking of striking, and Nicholas had been trying to stop that from happening. In the union everyone would strike together, and he was quite happy at Marlborough Mills. Nicholas was very concerned about all the workers, even the ones at other mills. Nicholas, while working for Mr. Thornton, had learned to hope that things might improve in time, but Slickson was bound to mess it all up with his cruelty and demands of the workers. Even the masters could suffer from his actions. Nicholas noticed that more of the men had noticed Slickson coming into the pub and none of them looked happy to see him. A majority of them had lost their jobs because of the Civil War, and Slickson had been the first one to cut jobs in order to still see some profit for himself. Masters never ventured into the slums and most certainly didn't mix with the workers. It was far too dangerous for the masters.

Slickson has really made a mess of it now. It won't be long before the men start to overcome him, thought Nicholas as he set his mug onto the table.

As a committeeman, Nicholas had to do something, and quickly. The workers around him started to stand up, and Templeton looked ready for a fight. With several pints of whiskey in him, Templeton had pure hatred shining from his eyes. Nicholas placed a hand on Templeton's arm and said, "Don't do something you will end up regretting later, Templeton." Templeton rounded the table, pushing away Nicholas's hand as he headed straight for Slickson, ready to fight. Nicholas looked over to the pub owner and motioned for him to send for the inspectors. Realizing he wouldn't be able to stop what was about to happen, he headed for the door and told the pub owner he was going for Mr. Thornton. Nodding, the pub owner sent his son Jasper, who was only seven, to get the inspectors and went back around the counter to wait for the inspectors.

Jasper reached Inspector Mason just as he was leaving a shop. "Inspector, Master Slickson has come drunk to the Golden Dragon and a brawl has broken out. My father has sent me to get you at once."

Blowing his whistle, Mason motioned to two young inspectors to follow him to the Golden Dragon. As they were approaching him on the sidewalk, he grabbed Jasper by the hand and headed to the Golden Dragon with the others.

Meanwhile, Nicholas had arrived at the mill and was knocking on the front door when Sarah answered it. "Miss, I must speak to the master at once," said Nicholas. Leading him down the hallway to the sitting room, Sarah announced Nicholas. John looked up from the book he was reading and asked, "What is it, Nicholas? What brings you out so late?"

Hannah and Margaret stopped working on their needlepoint and looked up as well. "It's Slickson, Master. He has come to the Golden Dragon drunk and has incited a brawl. You must come at once."

"Oh, John, do be careful!" said Margaret, walking with the men to the door.

John touched her cheek and said, "It's going to be fine. But I can't imagine what that fool man was thinking going into the slums at this time of the evening." He then kissed her forehead, and the men left.

Margaret walked to the window and looked down at them as they drove off. Hannah, who had already gone to the window as Margaret was walking the men out, looked sideways at her with concern. "I'm afraid that the masters and the workers are never going to see things the same way," said Margaret.

Finally arriving on the street to the pub, Nicholas got out and started running to the pub. John cautiously looked around as he climbed out of the carriage and asked the driver to wait for him. The lonely streets weren't lighted very well in this area, and he couldn't help but think that someone might be watching his every move. He made his way to the pub, looking back over his shoulder several times when he thought he heard some noise. Nicholas was inside standing over someone as John pushed his way through the crowd that had gathered.

Walking over to where Nicholas was standing, Inspector Mason had his back to John as he asked several men what exactly had happened. Looking down at the bloodied man lying on the floor, John realized that Nicholas and he had arrived too late. Slickson had been beaten to death by some of the workers. The pub owner, who had ducked down behind his counter, had regrettably not seen who had dealt the final blow. The inspector gathered several men together and was asking for some answers, but the workers were sticking to their story that they had not seen a thing.

John, wanting answers to those questions as well, asked Nicholas what he had seen before he had left the pub. Nicholas said he had not witnessed the brawl, as he had left right away to get John. The coroner arrived to get the body, and John left to notify Slickson's family about his death after telling Higgins to keep his ears open for any news on what had happened.

Arriving at Slickson's home, John knocked on the door. A slender man answered. John told him he was there to see Slickson's wife. Amanda was sitting in the sitting room working on a quilt. She looked up as John entered. "Hello, John," said Amanda, smiling up at him. "To what do I owe this honor? You never come here. If you are looking for Silas, he is not here at the moment."

"Yes, I know. I have come to give you some bad news, Amanda," said John. "Silas was beaten to death tonight at a pub in the slum area." John paused for her reaction. She looked down at her quilt and thought of their children. How would she tell them? He may have been a brutal man to her, but he had adored his children. John stood there, waiting for her to say something. Finally, she looked up; on her face was relief.

"Thank you so much for coming to tell me," said Amanda. "I need to go tell the children … actually I probably should wait until morning and not wake them at this late hour. Hamlet, please show Mr. Thornton out. I will get in touch with our barrister tomorrow. He can arrange everything."

After John left, Amanda started crying. Onlookers would have thought she had lost a part of herself after finding out about Silas, but she was actually crying with relief. She had been forced to marry Slickson four years earlier by her family who had thought she could solve all their financial woes by marrying a master. He had been a brute to her and in their bed. She had conceived four children during their marriage but had only given birth to two of them because of his constant beatings. He had treated her no better than he had treated his workers, and personally, Amanda was glad to be free of him. All his wealth would stay with her and the children. She would be well provided for the rest of her life. Her brother, who lived nearby, could run the mill's finances for her, and she would be able to stay in their home for the rest of her life. Her brother also would be able to help her if she should need it.

The next morning, Amanda had all the arrangements finalized and had Slickson buried before the day was done. The children were crying the entire time, and Amanda showed extreme courage by standing by her children throughout the day and coming to their comfort. Margaret, knowing how Amanda's life had been, was there to support her, offering to take the children for a while that day while Amanda attended to everything she needed to, which included having John organize the papers for her brother-in-law to start running the mill for her. He was a lot nicer man to her then Silas had been. He could start the next day.

CHAPTER 16

John had just sat down and was having Nellie pour him some coffee when Jane entered with a letter from the post. Laying it down on the table next to him, Jane went to clean the bedrooms. John picked up the letter and looked at it. It was addressed to him from a Lieutenant Blake from Liverpool.

Opening it, John frowned as he began to read.

Dear Mr. John Thornton,

I am writing to you from my sickbed. I have been fighting an unknown illness for several years and have gotten increasingly sicker as the years have passed. I will now get to the point of this letter. I believe you are married to a Margaret Hale, whose brother Frederick was on a ship with me. I worked with Frederick and some other men under the leadership of Captain Reid on *The Orion*, though at that time he was not yet a captain. Later on, I was with the captain on *The Russell*. I can attest to everything that Captain Reid did to the young men on those ships and especially to Frederick's abuse. The captain greatly disliked Frederick for being so efficient at his duties, and I personally witnessed him using a cat-o'-nine-tails on several of the young men. I witnessed a man fall to his death while trying to grab a rope to save himself from a flogging. I was one of the men put off the last ship with the captain. I was too scared of him to stay with the young men who decided to stay on board the ship. Frederick and those other men only did what I wish I had been brave enough to do. The captain would threaten us all. I'm sorry to say that he threatened to accuse us with terrible crimes if we didn't support him in what he was doing. Being the captain of the ship, we thought he would be believed over all of us. But now that I am soon to die, I want to clear my conscience. I am ashamed for not stepping forward before now. I ask that Margaret be brought to see me as soon as possible because I have information to give her about Frederick and an acquaintance of hers by the name of Henry Lennox. The doctors say I only have a few more weeks to live, so please come as quickly as you can. It is of great importance for her to come see me at once concerning her brother and the information about the captain of Frederick's ship.

Sincerely, Lieutenant Blake

Folding the letter back up, John stood and walked to the window of the sitting room to think over what he had just read. It was getting late, and John wanted to think about how he was going to approach Margaret with this information. He would talk to her tomorrow about it. Putting the letter on his desk in the study, he went upstairs to bed. Margaret had gone to bed exhausted from a day of shopping an hour earlier, and he didn't want to disturb her, so he went to a guest room for the night. He knew that she needed her rest for the baby as well as for herself.

The next morning when Margaret entered the sitting room, John was standing looking out the window on the yard below. He was clutching in his hand the letter he had received the day before. Hearing her enter the room, he turned to face her. "I received a letter yesterday from a Lieutenant Blake. He was on the ship with your brother Frederick. He has requested that you come see him. He is dying and has some vital information concerning both Frederick's sufferings by the hand of the captain and of your friend, Henry Lennox. From the tone of his letter, I'm wondering if Henry was truthful with you about being able to help Frederick."

Margaret gasped and clutched her mouth. "What do you mean?"

"I mean that this man will back up Frederick's story about the captain and has talked to Henry before apparently," said John. "Are you ready to take a journey to see this man, Margaret?"

"Yes, of course, I am. When shall we leave?"

"I thought this afternoon if all the arrangements can be made. You will need to get packed, and I need to have the mill looked after in my absence. Mother isn't going to be able to help much because of helping with Peter. I, will talk to Nicholas and have him run things for me along with Finn, of course. I think it is about time I started giving Nicholas more money for his work. He is always helping me out and not asking for much in return."

Margaret went to get Sarah to pack her things and to have Nellie get some food ready that they could take with them on the trip. It would be a bit of a train ride, and she didn't want to have cravings along the way. She always seemed to be hungry now. There would be some food provided on the train, but this way she wouldn't get too hungry. John exited the room to go to the mill and talk with Nicholas and Finn. There was some new equipment coming in soon, two new jennies. John knew Nicholas would know how to get them put in properly as well as oversee the men's division of equipment and workers. Finn would watch over the ladies and children and make sure the cotton orders were filled as required and shipped to the companies they needed to go. Mary would be running the food service, and he wanted to make sure there was money left for her to operate all the services from buying food to dispensing it to the workers. After the arrangements were made, John returned to the house to have his things packed for the trip. They told Hannah good-bye and set out in the carriage for Outwood Station. Several people were milling around at the shops along the way. One little boy was throwing a stick for his dog to chase as their carriage wove in and out of the people walking along the sidewalks and across the thoroughfares. *Brown's drapery store is seeing some business today*, thought Margaret as she gazed out the window. John, meanwhile, was going through some papers he had brought with him from the mill. They soon arrived at Outwood Station, and a young boy who had been standing by carried their bags to the train. John paid him in some coins and then followed Margaret onto the train. John, noticing an extra bag, asked Margaret what was in it.

Blushing a little and smiling, she said, "It's extra food in case I get hungry. I have been so hungry lately."

John laughed. "You have a big appetite now, do you? I can't believe it! I can't imagine why? What's wrong with you? Are you pregnant or something?"

Margaret playfully punched him in the arm and said, "I can't help it. I'm just always hungry. I'm afraid I'm going to be as big as a ship by the time this baby is born."

"Well, at least you have your appetite back. It was rough there for a while. I thought you might never have your appetite back," said John, looking less concerned.

Most of the trip was uneventful. Margaret slept a lot, and John had time to work on some papers. He didn't seem to notice how much Margaret was actually sleeping or even worry about why she might be sleeping so much, except for the fact that she was pregnant. Pulling into Liverpool Station, the train came to a stop. John put his papers in his bag and tapped Margaret on the shoulder. "We have arrived." She looked up at him through sleepy eyes. Rubbing them, she sat up.

"Do you know where Lieutenant Blake lives?" asked Margaret.

"His address is on the letter he sent. I figured we could ask someone here at the station and find out how to get there," said John.

The first attendant they came up on John asked how to get to the address on the letter. Then, after finding a carriage, they headed for Lieutenant Blake's home. The streets looked something between the fine streets of London and the shabby streets of Milton. Some of the streets seemed fine while others looked rather shabby. They had traveled for about a half hour when they pulled up in front of the house. It looked fine with steps like the ones on Aunt Shaw's home. Stepping out of the carriage and going up the steps, Margaret waited while John rang the doorbell. An elderly man answered the door and let them in, guiding them to a formal sitting room. The butler told them to remain there while he went to check on the lieutenant.

Coming back into the room several moments later, Simmons, the butler, was pushing a wheelchair with the lieutenant in it, who told Simmons to bring in some tea for his guests. Simmons once again entered the room and found everyone sitting around and talking.

"Master, if that is all, I will go see to the dinner arrangements," said Simmons.

"Yes, that will be all," said Lieutenant Blake, waving Simmons out of the room. "Now I must say, Mrs. Thornton, you look a lot like your brother. I can see you both have the same eyes." Lieutenant Blake touched her hand. "This must have been a tiresome journey for you in that condition."

Smiling, Margaret replied, "It was tiring, but if you have information about Frederick and that dreadful captain and how he treated Frederick, it has not been a wasted trip for us."

Looking from Margaret to the lieutenant, John asked, "What is the information you have for us?"

Looking at Margaret, the lieutenant replied, "I have all the documentation and logs that were kept on the ship. It contains all the incidents that happened there. The captain gave them to me for safekeeping and then doctored another set of logs to show to the authorities when he was confronted about the accusations made by your brother and the other men on the ship. I'm sorry to say, at that time I was too scared of the captain and what he might do to make problems for him." Rolling his chair to his desk, he opened a drawer and pulled out a logbook with the ship's name embossed on the front. Returning to Margaret's side, he handed it to John and said, "Look at all the dates of the incidents on that ship. It's a shame what those poor lads had to go through at the hand of the captain. Of course, I had already written you about the lad who fell to his death."

John opened the logbook and started glancing over the entries and dates. Every once in a while he pointed out a particular incident to Margaret as she nodded and said something.

Meanwhile, as they were looking over the book, the lieutenant went to his bookshelves and pulled down a box sitting on the third shelve. Going back to his desk, he opened the box and took out some letters. Glancing through them, he separated three letters from the others and placed all the others back into the box. Glancing up, he saw John and Margaret discussing how they could use the information to get Frederick pardoned by the admiral of the navy. He picked up the letters and went back to where they were sitting. "I think you might find these of use as well." He handed the letters to Margaret.

"They are addressed from Henry Lennox!" said Margaret, looking at John in surprise. Opening the first one, she started reading it out loud.

Dear Lieutenant Blake,

I have thought about the information you sent to me concerning Mr. Frederick Hale, and although it included information about the problems between the captain and Frederick, I don't believe it is enough information to warrant me to go forward with any action at this time. Ms. Margaret Hale, Frederick's sister, is in a very sensitive state at this time, having just recently lost both of their parents. It is best to not involve her in any of this information at this time. I will be in touch with you at a later date if I feel that there should be more investigating necessary on this matter. Personally, I feel that this information wouldn't help Frederick at this particular time.

Sincerely,

Mr. Henry Lennox

"I can't believe that Henry would withhold such important information from me!" said Margaret, as tears began to fill her eyes. "I have been betrayed by someone I thought cared a great deal for me. After all, he had asked me to marry him, had he not?"

John wiped away her tears. "You never told me he had asked you to marry him! When was this?"

"It was before we came to Milton. I had made a comment at Edith's wedding about what kind of wedding I would want, and he mistook it for a sign that I cared that way for him. But I never cared for him in that way at all, although it would have been a good marriage for me because of his financial situation. I turned him down." Margaret looked at John with love in her eyes.

The other two letters were correspondence between the captain and a friend stating ways that he was making the young men suffer at his very hands. Looking back at the lieutenant, John said, "Thank you so much for helping Margaret's brother. You'll never know how much it means to us both." He then shook the lieutenant's hand. Simmons came into the room to announce that dinner was served, and they all left to go to dinner.

That evening, as John and Margaret were getting ready for bed, John said, "When we get back to Milton tomorrow, I will start working on getting Frederick pardoned by the admiral of the navy. There has to be a way of handling this. I will not stop until we have found a way to get him back here to see you without any threat of something happening to him. He can bring Delores, his new wife, and Victoria, our niece, with him."

CHAPTER 17

Dr. Murray was bending over Margaret as she lay on the examination bed. Her back had been bothering her more and more every day. She could tell she had gained a good amount of weight over the last couple of months, maybe because she was always eating because she was always hungry. She was now five months along in her pregnancy. Lying on the bed was a great relief to her back. John stood to the side looking on as the doctor continued to listen to Margaret's stomach and chest.

"Why is she getting so big? She is a lot bigger then Fanny was! Her back is always hurting her," John stated.

Margaret looked over at John and frowned. "So the truth comes out. You think I'm huge, don't you? You did this to me, you know! This is your fault!" said Margaret, wincing at the pain in her back.

John's face softened as he looked at her. "I didn't mean you were huge. I just was thinking about how Fanny looked when she was pregnant, that's all. I'm just concerned."

Dr. Murray straightened up and finished his exam. He said, "Well, I know this seems unusual, but from what I can tell, I wouldn't be a bit surprised to be delivering two babies instead of one when the time comes. I believe I heard two heartbeats in there. Congratulations! I think there will be two little ones soon." Smiling, he shook John's hand.

Shocked, John's mouth dropped open. He slowly looked over at Margaret, who looked as shocked as he did. Finally, she said, "Well, that explains why I'm always hungry." Looking at John, she said, "See, what you did to me?" rubbing her stomach and laughing. "If you think I'm tired now, John, wait until the babies come. I will be dead on my feet. But I'm thrilled with the thought of it!"

John suddenly got a wide smile on his face and leaned to Margaret and hugged her. "Twins! Oh my. Two babies! I can hardly believe it! I love you so much for giving me such a precious surprise"! He kissed her forehead and spoke so only she could hear him.

Dr. Murray shook John's hand again and told him to watch her carefully so she didn't overdo it and have the babies too soon. Dr. Donaldson came in and congratulated them both. Margaret carefully stood up and got on her cover. It had started to get chilly with the wind blowing a lot and snow flurries once in a while. Getting into the carriage, Margaret turned to John and said, "If one of the babies is a girl, I want to name her Fanny."

John's eyes started to tear up. He put his hands on her face and pulled her forehead to him before kissing it again. "I couldn't love you more, my dear. You are my whole world. My mother is going to be so pleased. It would be a perfect tribute to my sister and her life," he said.

Margaret leaned back to look up into his eyes and wiped away the tear on his cheek with her finger. "I loved your sister. Nothing would make me happier than to name our child after her and to show you how much I care for you."

They continued the rest of the trip just holding each other while watching the people moving outside the window going on with their lives, clueless as to what had happened that day. They basked in their knowledge of their babies as they arrived in the yard of Marlborough Mills where everyone was busy.

As Margaret stepped from the carriage, she saw Hannah standing in her customary spot at the window, looking down on them. As they entered the house, Hannah turned from the window and watched them approach the sitting room. "What did the doctor have to say about your back?"

John looked at Margaret and said, "It appears that the pain in her back is to be expected since we are not having one baby, but two!" Grinning, he went to hug his mother.

Hannah patted his shoulder and looked at Margaret in surprise. "I can hardly believe it! Are you ready for that, Margaret?"

"I can hardly believe it myself, but I'm ready for whatever may happen," said Margaret, smiling at her. "And if one of the babies is a girl, we want to name her Fanny."

Hannah's eyes filled with tears. "That is the most beautiful surprise I have heard in a long time." Hannah went to Margaret and hugged her for the third time since she had married John almost a year and half earlier. Their lives were finally dealing them some well-deserved joy after all the months of sorrow and despair from the deaths of family members and workers at Wilson's mill.

For over a month, John had been discussing Frederick's case with the admiralty and other barristers around London and Edinburgh. From the testimony of Lieutenant Blake, who had finally died and several others, those who were found to have known what exactly had happened on the ships had charges brought against them by the admiralty. It was something that had never been heard of before, but the evidence had been substantial. John had written Frederick and told him of his pardon by the admiralty and the restoration of his name to good standing and honor on the list of navy men.

One month later, upon returning from the doctor's office, Margaret and John were in the sitting room with Hannah when there was a knock on the door. When Sarah opened it, standing there was a young man with a lady and a small child.

"Yes, sir. What is it you need?" asked Sarah.

"I am here to see Mrs. Margaret Thornton," said the young man.

"Stay here, sir. I will check to see if she is expecting visitors." Sarah started to close the door.

Putting his hand on the door, the man said, "She isn't expecting me, but she will be glad to see all of us."

"Hold on, please" said Sarah, frowning at him. She closed the door and went to the sitting room. "Excuse me, Mrs. Margaret, but there is a young man at the door with a lady and a child asking to see you. He is most urgent about it."

"Show them in," said Margaret. John and Hannah looked at each other. Soon, Sarah arrived in the sitting room followed by the young man, the lady, and child. Margaret put her hand to her mouth as she gasped loudly and then exclaimed, "Oh, my Frederick! Why didn't you write to tell me you were coming?" She walked over and put her arms around his neck. Then she introduced him to Hannah and John, whom Frederick thanked for helping him get pardoned.

Frederick turned to the lady at his side and introduced her. "This is Delores, Margaret." He hugged Delores at his side and then pointed to the child and said, "This is our daughter, Victoria. She is a hand full!" He smiled down at the little girl.

"Welcome to our home! Won't you please have a seat?" Hannah motioned for them to sit and told Sarah to set up some rooms for them.

"There is so much to catch up on. I am so glad to finally be back here to see you, Margaret," said Frederick, taking her hand and kissing it.

Hannah had Nellie bring in some tea. Victoria wanted to explore the room, as she saw some paintings on the wall and some statues of the Thornton family. Sarah walked around with Victoria as she explored the room. Delores sat next to Frederick and started talking to Hannah about embroidery and stitching. Soon the day seemed to have escaped them all as they sat down to dinner and Frederick and John started talking business. Margaret turned her attention to Hannah and Delores, who had been getting acquainted throughout the day.

"Delores, what do you think of England? It is quite different from Spain, I suppose," said Margaret.

"Yes, there are quite a few differences. But I know I will love it here since this is where Frederick is from," said Delores, smiling.

Margaret, Delores, and Hannah tittle-tattled for the rest of the evening while the men went to the billiard room to talk.

"Tomorrow, I will take you to meet Watson. He is my brother-in-law. He was Fanny's husband," said John to Frederick as they started to turn in for the evening. Victoria had fallen asleep on a nearby chair. Frederick picked her up as he and Delores told everyone good night and left for their rooms. John came over to Margaret and gave her a hug. "Frederick is a nice man. You have a nice brother there. Mother, we are turning in." He guided Margaret to the door of the sitting room.

"Good night then, you two," said Hannah as she finished her tea and then headed up to her room as well. Looking back into the sitting room, she thought about how happy she was to have such a full house of people around her. Margaret and John were now her whole life. They meant everything to her since she lost Fanny such a short time ago. Now that Frederick and Delores were here as well, life was going to be lively around the house.

The following week, Frederick, Delores, and Victoria arrived back to the house from town after looking for a home for their family. They had found a lovely one not too far from Marlborough Mill. Although Margaret would miss them, it was nice that Delores and Frederick would have their own place. It was on a side thoroughfare. Delores had wanted to get some fabric from the drapery store while they were out. She had a plan to make an outfit for her future nephews or nieces. They were smiling and laughing as they entered the sitting room.

"Margaret, what did the doctor have to say about your pains?" asked Frederick.

"We're having twins, as you well know," said Margaret, smiling and shaking her finger. "It was just a checkup anyway."

"Oh my. Are you excited?" asked Delores, acting all innocent.

Margaret just laughed. Frederick walked over to John and shook his hand. "Way to go! Twins! I'm surprised you didn't tell us more quickly about that when we first arrived here."

"Margaret was too excited about your arrival to say anything right away," said John. Victoria didn't understand all the excitement and wanted to know what was going on.

CHAPTER 18

For the past two months, Margaret had been on bed rest. She was starting to get bored sitting still all the time. She had made every conceivable thing a baby could wear while laying or sitting in bed. She had read thousands of books it seemed and had gotten visits from all of her friends, including Nicholas and Mary. Mary was now being seen in the company of Dr. Murray a lot and was having hopes of someday not working at the mill anymore, perhaps becoming an assistant nurse and assisting Dr. Murray in his duties. After all, she had taught Jenny everything she knew about cooking for the workers at the mill, so Jenny could take that job on if Mary were to move in another direction. Dr. Murray, being from Scotland, had learned the hard way about the dangers workers can face, which is why he cared so much about helping others. He was kindhearted and absolutely amazing to watch at work, Mary thought. He was gentle in his handling of his patients and showed a caring ability, which was not often seen by a doctor. He was in high demand by his patients. He had advanced quickly and had quite amazed Dr. Donaldson with his abilities and how fast he had learned them. Margaret could understand why Mary was so drawn to him. He had the capacity to turn the heads of almost any woman. They would follow him anywhere. His kindness was a very rare thing in this time of extreme poverty, strife, and crime brought on by the high unemployment of so many workers caused by the American Civil War and lack of cotton. Margaret had seen Dr. Murray with some of the child workers from the mills. He not only did his medical duties, but he would also lend a hand to any of their families when the children became sick from the circulating cotton fibers. Margaret had even seen him with one of Boucher's children who was dying from consumption. Dr. Murray had held her hand and told her that he would carry her spirit and strength with him and would use her memory for the strength to do the things he needed to for other people. When she looked into his eyes, Margaret could tell that she wished she had been his child instead of his patient. He just overflowed with kindness for others, which made him the perfect doctor. Margaret smiled to herself, thinking about him. Next to John and Frederick, he was the man she held in the highest esteem. She was glad he would be the one delivering her babies when they finally arrived.

John came in to check on her before he went back to the mill. He had come home for his tea break. Margaret looked up as he entered the room. "How has your day gone?" asked Margaret, noticing his tired expression.

"I had to lay off about twelve workers today. I was hoping it wouldn't come to that, but we have to make a profit. I have to use Egyptian cotton instead of cotton from America, and the cost of Egyptian cotton is more, so I have to cut some of our costs. Now I risk the possibility that the orders won't be filled on time because of it, but I want to keep the payroll safe." He bent down to kiss her on the forehead. "I have got to get back to my office. I will check in on you later." John left just as Hannah entered the room.

"Take care of yourself, John. You are looking tired," said Hannah. "I will. Don't worry about me so much, all right?" said John.

Mary arrived to see Margaret and nodded to John as he left. "I want to talk to you about something." Mary sat down beside Margaret's bed.

"All right. What is it?"

"As you probably have heard, I have been seeing Dr. Murray for a while now. I have formed a genuine affection for him. I can only describe it as the deepest love I have ever felt for any man," said Mary.

"Oh, I am so happy for you both, Mary! He is a very kind and generous man and would make the best companion I could ever imagine for you. He will never be really wealthy, but he will be a great match for you. Does he know how you feel?"

"Yes, in fact, that is why I am here. He has asked me to marry him." Mary eyes started to tear with joy.

Just then, Nicholas came into the room. "Have you told her yet, Mary?" "Yes she has, Nicholas. I am happy for your whole family. This really needs to be celebrated. Dr. Murray has been to see me often and didn't once hint at the fact that he was courting my friend or even that they had been courting for a while. I had to hear about it from the servants. I am going to say something to him the next time I see him," said Margaret, smiling.

"Mary wanted to know if you would be her bridesmaid since Betsy is gone." Nicholas glanced at Mary, who was looking shy. Nicholas started tearing a little at the thought of Betsy not seeing her sister's wedding. They both looked at Margaret with hope-filled eyes.

"If I am doing well enough to be off bed rest by the time of the wedding, I would love to do it," said Margaret, glancing down at her growing stomach. "Are you sure that you want a ship in your wedding party?" she laughed.

"You are not a ship. You look beautiful to us," said Mary, patting Margaret's hand. "We are getting married in a month at the church where your wedding was held."

"Well, your Dr. Murray said if I'm a good patient for the next couple of weeks, I may be able to do little things again and get off bed rest until the week before the babies are due. They are due two weeks after your wedding."

Later that evening, John came into eat dinner and got the story from Margaret and Hannah. "I'm happy for them both, but I'm not sure about you being in the wedding, Margaret," he said.

"Dr. Murray said I may be able to get off bed rest soon. I can hope, can't I?" asked Margaret, pouting a little.

John laughed. "All right, you win. If Dr. Murray allows you off bed rest, I guess it will be all right for you to be in the wedding party." John looked down at her stomach.

"I see what you're looking at. Mary said she doesn't care how big my stomach gets before the wedding, so I'll be all right with it too, I guess," said Margaret.

The next morning, Margaret asked Sarah to get Dr. Murray to visit her after he saw his patients. In the afternoon, he knocked on the door to the house, and Sarah went to answer it. Margaret called to her to bring him into her room. "Dr. Murray, I understand that congratulations are in order," said Margaret as Hannah walked into the room.

"Dr. Murray, why are you here? Is there something wrong with Margaret? You were supposed to come over tomorrow to check on her," said Hannah, alarmed.

"She sent Sarah earlier today to tell me to come over after I saw all my patients," said Dr. Murray, looking at Margaret.

"I wanted to find out about you and Mary. When did you start courting each other?" Margaret smiled up at him.

"Well, I want to hear this too." Hannah took a seat next to Margaret. "Actually, we first met at her home when Emma died. We started seeing

each other in passing here at the mill, my office, and other places. Soon we began talking to each other and finally got to know each other more when Fanny died at the reception after the funeral that was held here. I was afraid at first about what people would think of our relationship, seeing that she worked at the mill and I was an up-and-coming doctor. But doctors have the ability to socialize with both upper and lower society, so when she started volunteering at the clinic, I just couldn't resist her kindness to others and we started meeting in community places." He noticed Hannah's intake of breath. "I can reassure you, Mrs. Thornton, that nothing inappropriate ever happened that we should be ashamed of."

"You must know that a lady doesn't meet with a man unescorted. It just isn't done in polite society," said Hannah, concerned about what people would think of Dr. Murray after rumors of this got out.

"Well, her father was usually there, and since we aren't hiding our feelings anymore and everyone knows about the engagement, it no longer would apply anyway. Mary is the kindest, most giving person I have ever had the pleasure to meet, excluding you ladies, of course," said Dr. Murray, smiling. "Now since I am here, why don't I check and see that everything is good with you and the babies."

Sarah came into the room with tea and told Dr. Murray that he had received a message from Dr. Donaldson to go over to one of the worker's homes. A child was having difficulty breathing because of a fall from a tree in the cemetery. "Well, Margaret, you seem to be fine, so I will leave to meet Dr. Donaldson. I won't be able to partake of the tea, if you don't mind." Sarah showed him out.

"Well, Margaret, what are your thoughts about what Dr. Murray just told us?" asked Hannah.

"Honestly, I feel really happy for them, although I think they both should have thought about her reputation a little more. I hope that none of the servants heard anything because this could get out and ruin her wedding plans. People might start thinking she has to get married because she is pregnant or sullied and has been meeting him alone in private places as well." Margaret watched as Hannah rose to check on the progress of supper.

One week later, Mary was back at the house showing Margaret her wedding dress and bonnet. They were very simple, with no lace, flowers, or beads on them. The dress was made of simple cotton fabric with muslin trimming on the underskirts.

Margaret reached over to her side table and opened a drawer. "Mary, I want you to have this ribbon for your bonnet. And in that trunk over there is some lace left over from my wedding dress that you can use for your dress." Margaret handed the ribbon to her.

"Mrs. Margaret, I can't take these," said Mary, caressing the lace and ribbon, admiring the details.

"Yes, you can because it is my gift to you for your wedding." Margaret closed Mary's hands around the lace and ribbon.

"Thank you so much. I will treasure them always," said Mary, tearing up. "Don't start crying now," said Margaret. "You will get the lace wet."

CHAPTER 19

One month earlier, as Dr. Murray was leaving his office, Mary had come in to ask if she could start helping in some way in the clinic. She said she had always wanted to learn about caring for people through nursing. Dr. Murray said if she would come in for several weeks and just watch how they handled the patients, he would then see if Dr. Donaldson would hire her on as a nurse assistant. Mary agreed and started coming in on days she normally helped in the food building at Marlborough Mills. Jenny covered for her for as long as necessary, and Nicholas said he could manage having only Jenny doing the cooking for a while. Also, more of the children, being of age to work at the mill, assisted Jenny so Mary could have this chance at a better job. Mary came in the afternoon and stayed until she was no longer needed by the doctors. She was a fast learner and within those first several weeks became quite efficient at helping with the patients. Nicholas started noticing a change in Mary. She became more outspoken, talkative, and sociable. She was a great help with the children who came in, and when mill workers came in, they felt more comfortable with Mary there. The time went by quickly.

One evening, as Dr. Donaldson was leaving on a call to a ladies home, Dr. Murray asked Mary to stay behind so they could talk. "I want you to know that you have really brightened up this clinic," he said. "The patients seem to feel more comfortable when you are in the room and seem to understand the instructions we give them on their medications and tonics. I have been really impressed with you and the skills you have shown. Even Dr. Donaldson has commented that he finds having you here at the clinic very refreshing."

"I have only followed what you both have been showing me to do," said Mary, smiling. Pausing, she then asked, "Was there something else you wanted to discuss with me? Because I have to get back to the house to get dinner ready for the family. The work shift ended early tonight, and they don't cook for everyone since it's the start of the weekend."

"Well, actually, I'm not sure how to say this, but I would really like permission to start courting you," stated Dr. Murray.

Mary covered her mouth and made a little sound. "I was afraid to let my feelings show because I wasn't sure how you might feel about me and I didn't want to have any false hopes because you are above me in society and status," said Mary, smiling through tears.

"You are exactly what I need in my life," he said, touching her hand. "Will your father approve?"

"Just ask him. I'm sure he will have no objections," said Mary.

"By the way, you can call me James." He kissed her hand and led her out of the office and into the street.

"Come by our home tomorrow night. You can talk to Father then," said Mary, smiling as she turned to head toward home.

Nicholas was coming through the door when Mary arrived at the house. "Why are you arriving back here this late?" asked Nicholas.

"Dr. Murray wanted to talk to me about something. He will be coming here tomorrow night to speak to you about something. He wouldn't say what," said Mary, hiding a smile as she turned to start the dinner. Moving the pots onto the stove and pulling out a sack of potatoes, onions, and carrots, she started peeling them for a stew.

"Work was a bear today. We had one of the spinning mules break down, and Mr. Thornton is going to have to call in someone to fix it because it was beyond my capabilities," said Nicholas, coming to the sink to wash his hands.

"I'm sure he will have it fixed as quickly as possible because he doesn't want the orders to be behind schedule now, does he?" said Mary, continuing her preparations.

Thomas and the other children came into the room after doing their work and went to wash up.

"I will set the table," said Jenny as she urged Thomas to watch the others.

Mary handed her the dishes and utensils and turned back to her job.

"I am really enjoying the clinic, Father. There is always something different that happens every day," said Mary. "Dr. Murray told me today that he and Dr. Donaldson are very glad I came there because the patients seem more at ease." Nicholas listened as she tittle-tattled about her work at the clinic. He started to doze off when he heard Mary saying, "Father, wake up. Dinner is ready, and your head is about to fall into your dish of stew."

Thomas and the others started to laugh. "Now, don't be laughing at how tired I am. Eat your dinner and go to bed," said Nicholas. "It is going to be a long day tomorrow because of the mule, so we will be working longer hours. You will need your rest to make it through the day, and so will I."

Soon after the meal, Nicholas said good night and left to go upstairs. The children went to bed as Mary washed up the last of the dishes in the sink.

John was standing at the window looking down on the workers arriving when Margaret came into the room.

"Do you have coffee or tea in you glass?" asked Margaret, walking to the window to touch his shoulder.

"Tea. Why don't we go over to the table? I was waiting for you to come down so I could talk to you," said John. "I have been thinking about Dr. Murray and Mary's wedding in two weeks. Are you sure you are going to be able to go?"

"Dr. Murray said that he would not be able to tell me if it will be all right until several days before the wedding. But if he says it will be all right, I plan on going, and no one is going to stop me." Margaret frowned at him. "Besides, I'm getting bored on bed rest all the time." She pouted a little.

John couldn't help but smile. "Well, if he says it is all right to go to the wedding, I will not leave your side during it then." He was making sure she understood he wouldn't budge on this point.

Margaret slowly smiled and said, "Thank you for understanding."

Dr. Murray arrived at the mill two weeks later to check on Margaret and was happy with her appearance and with the sound of the heartbeats of the babies, so he released her to go to the wedding in two days. But he stipulated that she would need to sit down often and not be on her feet a lot. Margaret happily agreed as Hannah and John told Dr. Murray that they would make sure she took it easy.

Mary arrived at the mill two days later about two hours before the wedding to have Sarah help her with her hair. Mary had chosen to wear pink flowers in her hair with ringlets down the sides of her face. The lace Mary had added to her dress made it look almost store bought.

Margaret came into the guest room to see how everything was going. When she saw Mary in her dress with her hair all fixed up, she almost started to cry. But instead she said, "Oh, Mary! You look so beautiful! Dr. Murray doesn't know what he is in for when he sees you walking down the aisle. You are going to take his breath away."

John arrived from the office to say that all the men were heading over to the church and that the ladies needed to hurry up because it looked like the weather may turn quite bad. Margaret met Hannah in the hallway and told her that they would be leaving in the carriage for the church soon. Margaret went to her room and put on her yellow dress that Mary had chosen for her to wear for the wedding and looked at herself in the mirror. She felt that she looked like a cow and yellow was not her color. But she was doing this for Mary. Sighing, she sat down on the bed and leaned down to put on her shoes.

"Uh, Sarah, I need your help. I can't get on my shoes because I can't reach my feet," said Margaret, sitting back up on the bed.

A few minutes later, Hannah came into the room. She had overheard Margaret calling for Sarah. She had come in to help Margaret because Sarah was still busy helping Mary get ready.

"Thank you, Hannah. I feel so huge now," said Margaret, frowning and sighing.

Hannah laughed and said, "Well, you do have two babies in there, you know. You look lovely, my dear. Being pregnant is a precious time. It will be over soon enough, and you will have two beautiful little children to hold in your arms." She finished tying the shoes. "You are ready now. It is time to leave for the church." Hannah gave Margaret her hand to help her stand. They walked down the hallway and collected Mary on the way out to the carriage.

Mary climbed in first and then Margaret. Hannah handed the flower bouquets to them both and then climbed in herself. Knocking on the side of the carriage, she called for the driver to head for the church.

The men were all standing outside, except for Dr. Murray, who was already standing at the front of the church, waiting for the ceremony to start. Hannah and Margaret climbed out of the carriage and entered the church. When everyone was in his or her spot, the music started, and Mary entered the church and walked up the aisle to the front for the ceremony. It was a beautiful wedding. Mary's siblings had decorated the sanctuary with wildflowers they had found along the edges of town. After the ceremony, everyone went down to the river to a grassy area for the reception. Both Mary and Dr. Murray looked very happy as they celebrated with Nicholas, the kids, and Dr. Murray's family, who had traveled from Scotland for the wedding. The weather ended up just drizzling, and it turned out to be a perfect day, with the sun shining through misty raindrops and finally stopping altogether.

One week later, Margaret was headed to the doctor's office for one last checkup when she felt something wet on her dress as she sat in the carriage. Hannah, who was with her, noticed a puddle on the floor of the carriage and looked up at Margaret in alarm as she realized that Margaret's water had broken. Hannah knocked on the carriage wall and called for the driver to speed up to the doctor's office. Upon arriving there, Hannah ran up the front steps to get Dr. Murray. He came running out to help with Margaret, who had started having pains by this time. He had just reached the carriage when lightning and thunder rumbled across the sky. Dr. Murray looked up at the sky and asked the driver to help him get Margaret out of the carriage. "This sky is going to break loose at any moment. We need to get her inside quickly."

The driver helped Dr. Murray lift Margaret out of the carriage and up the steps into the office. "Help me sit her on the examination bed," said Dr. Murray to the driver. When the driver turned to leave, Hannah grabbed his shoulder and told him to go back to the mill and get Mr. Thornton and bring him back to the doctor's office.

Hannah stood holding Margaret's hand while she struggled with her pains. Dr. Murray started feeling around on her abdomen and said, "I believe that this first baby is turned the wrong way. Mrs. Thornton, I need you to go get Dr. Donaldson, Mary, and the other nurse."

Hannah told Margaret she would be right back and left. Margaret struggled with another pain as Dr. Murray started pushing on her to try to turn the baby's body around. Finally, it felt like the baby moved some. About that time, the nurses and Dr. Donaldson arrived. Dr. Murray briefed Dr. Donaldson, and then they asked Hannah to wait in the waiting room while they took care of Margaret.

Margaret struggled to push the baby out, and after about an hour, the baby still hadn't been born. Now Margaret and the baby were both beginning to struggle, and the heartbeats were slowing down. John finally arrived at the office, as he had been delayed because of the heavy rain. The thunder and lightning hadn't helped either. One could hear the rain hammering on the roof of the office.

"How is she doing?" John asked Hannah as he came into the office.

"They haven't come out yet, but one baby has not turned the right way. They haven't said anything yet about the other baby. I have heard her call out several times now," said Hannah. John started pacing as he waited for someone to tell them what was happening.

Meanwhile, Dr. Murray was listening to Margaret's abdomen and explaining to Dr. Donaldson that the baby he had got to move a little was doing fine for now, as its heartbeat had gone back up. The other baby's heartbeat, however, was slowing down, and if they didn't do a procedure to deliver them quickly, both babies may not survive. Dr. Donaldson then listened to Margaret's abdomen and agreed with Dr. Murray's assessment.

"I will go tell Hannah and John what is happening and about the procedure. I will explain it to them the best way that I can," said Dr. Donaldson.

As he was leaving the room, dark fluid started coming out of Margaret. "Oh no. Tell them that we might end up with the babies being blind

because they have dirtied their sac water," Dr. Murray said. He had one of the nurses clean the area. "We won't know about the babies' eyes until after we deliver them."

In the waiting room, Dr. Donaldson took off his mask to talk to Hannah and John. "John, the first baby we had to turn a little is doing well, but we are going to have to get the babies out rather quickly.

They are just not coming as fast as they should be, and Margaret is struggling with the pains. One of the baby's heartbeat has slowed down too much and has put it in distress. There is also a possibility that they will be born blind because they have dirtied their sac water. So we are going to have to cut her abdomen to get the babies out quickly to save their lives. We will come back out when we are through to talk to you." Dr. Donaldson then left the room. John looked over at Hannah and started tearing up.

"John, they are all going to be all right. I just know it," said Hannah as she hugged her son.

"I can't go on without her. I don't exist without her anymore." John went and stood by Margaret's door.

Dr. Murray was getting the tools ready for the procedure as Mary wiped Margaret's forehead with a wet cloth. Picking up a bottle of banana wine, Dr. Murray washed his hands with it and then lifted Margaret's head and had her take a sip. He then gave Margaret something to bite down on as he rubbed some topical medicine on her abdomen to numb it as well as some of the banana wine to kill any bacteria. Dr. Donaldson tied down her legs and arms, and Mary held some water to Margaret's lips. Dr. Murray made his first midline cut and applied cautery to minimize hemorrhaging. Shortly after that, he pulled back the skin and started pulling out a baby. The first baby he pulled out, he handed to Mary, who sucked out its nose and mouth with a syringe and spanked its bottom. It looking kind of blue and wasn't breathing. She quickly breathed into its face several times and got a weak cry. She then turned it over on its back and patted it. The baby cried louder then, causing Dr. Murray to sigh with relief. Mary cleaned it up and handed the baby back to him. It was a boy. Dr. Murray then handed the baby to Dr. Donaldson to take to John. Dr. Murray quickly focused his attention back to the other baby and pulled it out and handed it to the other nurse while he started massaging Margaret's abdomen to make it contract. He pinned the wound with iron needles and covered it with paste from a green jar that was made with some African herbs that a doctor friend had given to him. Margaret was moaning now. She had dropped the bite stick. The other baby started crying right away.

Meanwhile, Dr. Donaldson was presenting John with his son. John looked down into his little face and lost his heart for the second time in his life. Here was his child, a little helpless creation Margaret had given him today.

The other nurse had cleaned up the wiggling baby girl. "You have a little girl and boy, Margaret." Mary handed her the baby girl, who she had just taken from the other nurse. Margaret felt weak but very happy as she looked down into the face of her daughter. Tears started pouring down her cheeks as she said, "Have you even seen anyone so beautiful and so perfect?" She kissed her daughter's little hand and smiled at Dr. Murray, who was cleaning up his tools and smiling over at her. The other nurse cleaned up Margaret's abdomen and legs, added bandages where needed, and covered her with a blanket, and then went out to the waiting room to get John and Hannah.

John walked into the room, holding their son in his arms. "Our son is so handsome, Margaret. Let me see our little girl now." He laid their son on Margaret's chest and took their daughter from her arms.

Margaret looked at her son and kissed his forehead. "Oh, John, they are simply wonderful! How can we feel so much love for something so small? My heart is just bursting with love I feel for them both." Margaret smiled up at John as he bent down to gently kiss her on the lips. Hannah held first one baby and then the other, too excited and in awe to speak. Dr. Donaldson came over to the babies and started checking their eyes. When Margaret asked him if they could see all right, he smiled and said that John and Margaret had two perfect babies, which was quite a miracle in this part of the country. John and Margaret smiled at each other as they did a huge family hug with the babies and Hannah. Mary hugged Dr. Murray as she watched John, Margaret, and their new babies. Finally, handing their daughter to Hannah, Margaret went to sleep from exhaustion, and they all left the room.

Two weeks later, Margaret was dressing little Fanny and Hannah was dressing little Richard for their christening. Margaret was marveling at how much they had already grown. Fanny was looking more and more like John, as she had her daddy's eyes, and Richard was looking a lot like Frederick when he was little. He had Margaret's eyes, though. Frederick, Delores,

Victoria, John, Watson, and Peter, along with Nicholas, Mary, the Boucher children, Dr. Murray, and Dr. Donaldson were all waiting downstairs for them. Mrs. Shaw, Captain Lennox, and Edith had even traveled from London for the christening, which had pleased Margaret. They were also downstairs waiting so they could all head over to the church together. Rebecca, Sarah, and Jane came to see if they needed any assistance.

"We are all ready," said Margaret, looking at her babies and admiring their outfits. Fanny was wearing Margaret's christening dress, which had been her great-grandmother's. Richard was wearing John's christening gown, which had been his father's before him. They all walked downstairs, and then everyone climbed into their carriages and headed for the church. The reception would be back at the house with only an intimate few, those who were the most dear in John and Margaret's lives. They were the ones who had waited downstairs for them. Margaret knew that everything had changed. That life would be forever changed by the birth of her children. No matter where life took her or her family, she would never regret coming to Milton, which she had finally given the chance to prove all the possibilities one could have from living in such a place. It would be her greatest lesson learned, that she should never judge a place based on what others feel to be true. Margaret looked around at everyone standing there in the church, her dearest family and friends. She knew they all would soon realize that their lives had just started on an adventure of a lifetime, and that this all was happening during a time of extreme poverty, chaos, and even some miracles. *And two of those miracles are right here*, she thought as she looked down into the faces of her babies.